Saddles & Secrets

Saddles & Secrets

AN ELLEN & NED BOOK

JANE SMILEY

Alfred A. Knopf

New York

Text copyright © 2019 by Jane Smiley
Jacket art copyright © 2019 by AG Ford

Visit us on the Web! rhcbooks.com

Educators and librarians, for a variety of teaching tools, visit us at
RHTeachersLibrarians.com

Library of Congress Cataloging-in-Publication Data
is available upon request.
ISBN 978-1-5247-1815-2 (trade) —
ISBN 978-1-5247-1816-9 (lib. bdg.) —
ISBN 978-1-5247-1817-6 (ebook)

The text of this book is set in 12.75-point Fairfield LH.
Interior design by Jaclyn Whalen

Printed in the United States of America
March 2019
10 9 8 7 6 5 4 3 2 1

First Edition

Saddles & Secrets

Chapter 1

After my lesson at Abby's ranch on Sissy, who is not as bad as she was in the spring, and can now even jump a little bit, Abby said that I had to learn something new, and I was sort of excited, but then the thing I was to learn was how to clean my saddle. I had to carry my own saddle into the tack room and put it on the saddle rack (I groaned a little so that Abby would know that the saddle was heavy, but she just laughed and handed me a sponge and a piece of soap that was blond and didn't smell anything like flowers). I watched her and did what she did—rubbed the sponge on the soap and then on the saddle and then on the soap and then on the saddle. She was fast. I was slow. And okay, I did close my eyes and let my mouth hang open a little so that she would think I was falling asleep, because one of the best ways to get through something boring is to make jokes.

While my eyes were closed, I thought maybe I really had fallen asleep, because I heard something I had never heard before, a deep, melodious voice singing, "From this valley they say you are going. We will miss your bright eyes and sweet smile." My eyes popped open, and I looked right at Abby, who didn't seem to hear a thing. The song went on, "For they say you are taking the sunshine that has brightened our pathway awhile."

Abby kept soaping.

I did, too. I listened to the end, and afterward there was silence, except for the soap soap soap. I finally said, "Did you hear something?"

"What?"

"A sad song."

"Oh, sure. 'Red River Valley.' That's one of his favorites."

"Who?"

"My dad. If he's in a good mood, he sings a sad song."

I said, "I never heard him sing before."

"Really?" She did not seem impressed. To me, it sounded like having a radio in your own barn. After a minute or so, she said, "He likes singing in the barn because the acoustics are good."

"What does that mean?"

"The walls and the ceiling make his songs sound richer."

"Don't you like it?"

"I do, but I hear it all the time."

I bent down and went under the rack, which is really just a two-by-four on some legs, and started soaping the other side of my saddle. Abby's dad is scary. He always wears a big cowboy hat pulled over his eyebrows, and when he isn't wearing it, like at lunch (I have stayed for lunch twice), his eyebrows go down over his eyes like they don't know any better, which makes him look angry. He also has a loud voice, but now that I've heard him sing, I think that might not be so bad. We soaped and soaped, then Abby went over to the hooks and got the bridles. I sighed. She smiled, but didn't say anything. I heard her dad start another song, but he went outside and was walking away, so I couldn't hear it anymore. "Red River Valley." Well, I have heard that song before. Grandma sings it under her breath sometimes, or hums it. I said, "Your dad singing that song was a once-in-a-lifetime experience."

Abby said, "Ellen, you are so funny. He'll be very glad to hear that."

We unbuckled all the buckles and took the bridles apart and cleaned them one strap at a time. We even used an old toothbrush to clean the bits. Afterward, I ran out of the tack room to the pasture, where Ned was standing by the fence. I gave Ned a bit of carrot that I had been saving for him, and then a little kiss on the nose. He wasn't mine yet, but we were taking baby steps in that direction, such small baby steps that no one had noticed them except me.

I am in fifth grade now. School started a month ago, and then, two weeks ago, it was Abby's birthday, and my mom and I went to the big department store where she used to work, and we pushed Joan Ariel down all the aisles and looked at all the stuff for sale. Mom worked for a long time in women's clothing, and for a short time in children's shoes and clothing, and also in kitchenwares. She knows the whole store. Every time I ask her, she says that she never worked in the toy department, but Grandma says that she did, she just doesn't want me to know, because then I will nag her.

Nagging is my absolute best talent, even though I call it "making my case." My dad likes this show on TV, *Perry Mason*. Perry Mason argues about everything and he always wins.

What we found for Abby was not a sweater, like Mom wanted, or a dinner plate with a longhorn cow on it, which Joan Ariel (I said) kept pointing at (Joan Ariel loves to point at things and go, "Ba ba ba!"), but an Instamatic camera. I saw it when we first walked into the store, because it was near the door, and I kept talking about it, and then in the end, Mom put her hands on her hips and said, "Well, okay then!" This is what Dad calls "the slow drip." You suggest something enough times, and they give in. The camera cost eighteen dollars, but Mom still gets her 20 percent discount, so, hello, Mr. Nathan, my fifth-grade teacher, that comes out to fourteen dollars and forty cents. I figured that out in my head. I spent my own money on two film cartridges, and maybe that will last her until Christmas. My plan is that she will take a lot of pictures of Ned.

I need a lot of pictures of Ned because I don't see him very often. Before this week, I hadn't seen him since August, and before that, I had only seen him twice since I rode him—well, got on him—in the spring on the day of the Kentucky Derby (that's my secret, and Ned's, too). Blue has been at the stables for five and a half months—all through the showing season. I keep telling Jane, who runs the stables, that he needs a break, but she just laughs at me and says that he is fine. And it is true that he is glossy and handsome and completely well behaved, like a saint, as my grandma would say. Ned hardly talks to me anymore, which makes me sad, and also makes me wonder if he ever talked to me at all.

I have an excellent imagination.

After we put the saddles on the saddle racks and the bridles on the bridle hooks, we went back outside. Abby said, "Isn't it such a beautiful day!"

I said, "When are you going to ride Ned?"

"How long are you staying?"

I looked at my watch. "About another hour. Dad is looking at cars. He loves to look at cars. I could stay all day and he wouldn't notice."

"My dad is like that about horses."

Another good thing about Abby's dad.

"Okay, I'll ride Ned now, and you can get on the

new pony. He's very easygoing, and I'm getting a little big for him."

"Are you giving me another lesson?"

"No. You're being my exercise rider."

Exercise riders are the ones at the racetrack who ride the horses early every morning, then the jockeys come out and ride them in the races. Sometimes an exercise rider gets to end up as a jockey, but most of the time, the exercise riders are too big to be jockeys. Jockeys are grown-up men who are maybe two inches taller than I am. I am 4'11" and wear a size five shoe. We had gotten measured that week. I said to Abby, "Did you get measured this week?"

"No. They don't do that in high school unless you're playing a sport, but I know how tall I am because I went to the doctor for my checkup. I'm five feet eight inches. He thinks I've stopped." She looked relieved. She is taller than her mom. I'm not taller than my mom. I wish I were.

By now we were at the pasture gate. The chain wraps around and around it because Abby's jumper, Gee Whiz, loves to open the gate and wander. He doesn't jump out of the pasture, though, which I don't quite understand, because the pasture fence is 4'6", and he can jump that high. If Ned were still talking to me, I would ask, but he isn't.

After we had taken Ned and the pony, whose name is Hot Potato, out of the pasture and wrapped the chain around the gate and the fence over and over (I saw Gee Whiz looking at us, too), I walked along behind Ned and watched him. I am sorry, but even though he is maturing (you never say "growing up" about a horse, because a horse usually gets to be his or her full height at two, which is like a teenager in human terms), he still reminds me of a puppy. I said this in front of him last spring, and he walked away like he would never forgive me, but what is wrong with a puppy? Puppies are always cute and everyone loves them; they are soft and rounded all over and do lots of things with their bodies. When Ned lies down to roll, he goes from one side to the other, which many horses can't do, and he also throws his legs around and wiggles. To me, that is like a puppy. All that I meant was, he reminds me of a puppy, but a beautiful puppy.

Hot Potato is a red roan Welsh cob. I said these words to myself after Abby said them to me. While we groomed Ned and Hot Potato, she told me all about him—he's sixteen years old, and he was imported from England when he was four and his English owners came to live near the stables. They showed him for a while, but the girl and then the boy grew out of him. He has since had two other owners, who also grew out of him, which is what happens with ponies. He's mostly sound but a little nippy, and Jane, at the stables, thinks that he needs some time with Abby and her dad, a little retraining after years of doing things his way. Abby said, "Keep your eye on him, and if he pins his ears and turns his head toward you, just present your elbow so that his nose hits it before he nips at you. That way, he will think it's his fault."

Abby and her dad think that horses do best when they punish themselves rather than when you punish them. I did what I was told because I didn't want to get nipped, but that meant that I couldn't pay much attention to Ned.

Until we were on them, and in the arena. Once we were in the arena, I could feel in my own body that Hot Potato was sighing and saying to himself, "Oh, this again; I know how to do this," and everything I asked him to do, he did. Abby watched us for a while, I guess to make sure we were getting along. We walked here and there, looking at the jumps and up the hill and over at the pasture, then we trotted some circles and loops, then we walked again, and then we cantered some figure eights. Hot Potato is a little chunky, or "heavyset," as my mom says, but he moved nicely, and his canter was loose and rhythmic. When I came down to the walk, Abby said, "I guess in England, some of them were used in coal mines, and they take them foxhunting. All sorts of things. I like him. I don't think he looks sixteen, but then, ponies live into their thirties."

I said, "Do they get bored?"

"Well, maybe that's his problem at this point. He's been good for too long."

That, I could understand.

Now Abby picked up her reins and began working Ned. Hot Potato and I stood quietly and watched for a while. Ned knows a lot more than he did in the spring, especially about going slowly and rating himself, which means controlling his stride and rhythm rather than just doing what comes naturally, which for Ned, and most racehorses, is going fast and stretching out. The first thing Abby did was walk and then trot around each of the fences, in loops and circles, then she walked on the bit, which means you are holding the reins tightly enough that you can feel attached to the horse's mouth, and then she walked on a loose rein, and even on the buckle. This lasted for maybe ten minutes, and looked good, and I thought that Ned was trained, but then I saw a funny thing, which was that he started pricking his ears and looking around and picking up speed. Abby tightened the reins just a little but kept going. Now Hot Potato pricked his ears and looked around, too—I felt him shift under me, so I started walking again. But almost immediately he stopped looking around and just kept walking. I didn't see anything, not even Abby's dog, Rusty, walking along the hillside. Everything was quiet.

Everything but Ned. Abby trotted some circles. Ned had his head up, but then he lowered it and went around properly, bending his body as if he knew where the circle was and that it had to run from his nose to his tail. He blew some air out of his nostrils, and then Hot Potato blew some air out of his nostrils, and I kicked him a little and we trotted along the fence line. At the gate, even though he was on a pretty loose rein, I got him to turn in a nice loop. I could see Ned and Abby at the far end of the arena. They had come down to the walk and now lifted into the canter, and they cantered along for four strides. Suddenly Ned threw up his head, tucked his hind end, and ran away, not as if he was mad or racing, but as if he was scared to death. Hot Potato watched him. I picked up my reins, because sometimes when one horse does something, the others decide to do the same thing, but Hot Potato is sixteen and Ned is four (which means, Mr. Nathan, that Hot Potato is four times as old as Ned), so Hot Potato stood quietly. Ned bucked and Abby shifted to one side before taking hold, bringing him down, and getting him to walk. They came over to us. He kept looking around. He was breathing hard. When they got to us, Abby said, "I do not know what we are going to do with this horse."

I said, in my own mind, "Ned, what is going on?"

Ned said nothing.

Chapter 2

When you come back to school in the fall, everything is different, even if you've been seeing the other kids over the summer. For example, my friend Ann and I would meet a couple of times a week, either down the hill from my house, at a little peninsula called Lovers Point, to look for seashells (Ann has a collection), or up the hill from the school to play tennis, which mainly meant trying to hit the ball back and forth over the net and hoping for the best. I was glad to get out of the house, and Mom was glad to be rid of me, so I didn't mind going, and I would imagine riding Ned up and down the hills or along the beach. And now Ann is back in my class this year, but at lunchtime on the first day of school, I came in late, and she was already sitting with two girls from her class last year, so I sat down with Melanie Trevor, who was alone, and then Ruthie Creighton crept in and sat with us. Todd sits with the boys, and he isn't in our class anyway. I maybe mind about Ann and maybe don't, since Melanie is the world's best student and most interesting person, and Ruthie still doesn't say much, but she smiles more than she used to and keeps her socks pulled up (I took her around behind the school on the second day and told her how to do it, and then I reminded her when she needed it for the next few days, and now she does it). Melanie does not do what I say—I do what she says— and Ruthie does what I say, and so we get along, and I can see across the lunchroom that Ann and those girls have little arguments all the time. Does Melanie like me? I have no idea. I didn't see her during the summer, because she goes to overnight camp for the whole time. She thinks I'm funny, and that's enough for her. It's a good thing that we sit at opposite ends of the second row of desks in Mr. Nathan's class, otherwise I might look at the answers on her papers. I see Jimmy Murphy doing that, but he must not learn anything, because she gets A's and he gets C's, and that is that.

As for Ruthie, things seem better at her house. She

brings her own lunch now, so maybe that's why she is willing to sit with us. Mom still tut-tuts when we pass her house pushing Joan Ariel in her stroller (Joan Ariel gets a lot of stroller exercise because Mom believes in fresh air), but last Sunday we stopped to admire a lemon tree in a pot at the bottom of the steps (Mom loves the smell of lemon blossoms), and a lady in a cap with a bucket came around the house. She and Mom went on and on about the lemons, and then the lady said that she was Ruthie's aunt, she was living with them now, she worked in the bakery at the market, and then they talked about Bundt cakes until Joan Ariel started fussing, because she would much prefer moving to sitting in one place. Then Ruthie's aunt, whose name is Mrs. Larsen, said what a cute baby, and so on, and we kept walking.

The summer went by very fast, even though I hardly saw Ned. I did get to show at the stables, on Blue, for three days, and even though it was gloomy and windy, I won a third, a fourth, and a first. The reason I won the first was that one of the jumps faced the forest, and horses from down south kept spooking at it even though it was 2'3", which is nothing. But Blue sees the forest a lot, so he knows there is nothing bad there. He jumped it perfectly every time, even when the wind came up as we were approaching it. Blue is a perfect example of how horses learn things and remember what they've learned, because he used to be very spooky. When I lie in bed the night after my lesson and think of Ned, I think, "Talk to Blue!" I can see the ribbons glinting in the moonlight, over by my dresser. Gee Whiz won a class, too, and I saw him, because it was the same day as my class, only in the afternoon, and Dad decided to leave me there all day with some money for a hot dog and an ice cream sandwich, and after my class was over, Abby let me wander around because I know enough now to stay out of the way.

Watching Gee Whiz jump is like watching a giant white bird—say, a pelican—fly. He usually likes to be dirty, but Abby had him so clean that day you could practically see yourself in his side like in a mirror (yes, I am exaggerating, but exaggerating is fun). He was the only white horse in his class, so compared with him, all the other horses, even the two chestnuts, seemed to canter around in a cloud, and then here he came, he coiled himself into a ball when he and Abby cantered their circle, then stretched out as they headed for the first jump, and then he launched himself. The woman next to me in the stands gasped, and yes, he is very large and he does seem a little out of control, but he didn't touch a single pole, and of the three horses in the jump-off, he was the only one to clear everything. And when I say "clear," I mean that I could see the clouds in the distance between his chest and the top of the fence. Sophia and her jumpers, Pie in the Sky and Onyx, weren't in the class, it was too low for them, but she was watching.

The other thing that happened over the summer was that my grandparents from Pennsylvania came for a visit, for two weeks, to see Joan Ariel for the first time. They also wanted to see everything else, so we went to all of the towns around here, to Abby's ranch, to some old famous houses, to one beach after another (but not to Disneyland), to museums and art galleries. It all seemed fine until the middle of the second week, which was two weeks before school started again, when I was sitting in my bed after dinner reading a book about a boy who goes to live by himself in some mountains. My window was open because I love the smell of the flowers, and I heard my dad and his dad step out onto the back porch. They were already talking. My dad said, "She'll never stand for that, and—"

Then his dad interrupted him and said, "You're much more likely to find something worth doing back east."

"I don't believe that. Anyway, this is our home."

"Really? Thirty years there, ten, twelve years here? Your mother misses you."

Dad coughed.

Pop (that is what he likes to be called) said, "I do, too."

Dad said, "I'll think about it. I do think about it, believe me."

Then they went in the house. But in the morning, I remembered what they had said, so of course I made my ears as big as I could and *stopped, looked, and listened* (this is something they have been telling us in school since kindergarten, especially about crossing the street). Mom was being very polite to Gran and Pop—big smiles that seemed stuck on her face for an extra moment or two—and giving them most of the scrambled eggs and all of the English muffins, then asking them four or five times what they wanted to do that day. Gran was smiling a lot, too, but also she would look over at Pop and wrinkle her eyebrows like she didn't understand what was going on. Finally, Mom got up and went into the kitchen, and Pop looked at Gran and shrugged a little bit. After that, everyone played with Joan Ariel like there was nothing else to do in the world, so I went outside and walked down the street. Mary Murphy, who is fourteen, had Brian out in their side yard, pushing him on the swing set. He would say, "Higher! Higher!" and Mary would heave and ho and bend like she was pushing harder and harder, but the swing only went a little higher. After a few minutes, Brian and I were both laughing, and then Mary started to laugh, too. Everyone, including Jimmy Murphy, says that once Jimmy went all the way over the top of the swing set, but there's a limb of a pine tree pretty close to the top, so I don't believe it. Mary said hi and asked me if Joan Ariel was crawling yet, and I said no, she would rather sit in one place and hold things in her hands and look at them.

"Lucky you," said Mary.

I said, "So does Brian start kindergarten this year?"

"No, his birthday is behind the line. He won't be five till December."

"What is he doing, then?"

"Arguing."

That made me laugh, too, and right then, Brian said, "I'm walking to the beach."

"You are not walking to the beach."

"I am!"

"You are too young to walk to the beach."

"I am not!" He raced toward me, to the gate, but I held it shut. When he got to it, he pushed against me twice, then stepped back, stuck his tongue out just a little, and sauntered over to the sandbox and sat down. "Saunter" is a word I just learned. It means to walk like you don't care about things. It was in a book I was reading and I looked it up in the dictionary. I love the dictionary.

Mary said, "Thursday's child has far to go."

I said, "Is Brian a Thursday's child?"

"No, I am." She sighed.

I said, "I am, too. I always thought that meant that I was going to see the world."

Mary smiled and said, "Well, let's hope so."

"What is Brian?"

"Sunday. Bonny and blithe and good and gay."

Another word to look up, "blithe."

Then she added, "We'll see."

I heard my name and turned around. Mom waved me back to the house.

When I got there, I said, "Why is everyone standing around?"

"Well," said Gran, "we haven't quite made up our minds what to do today."

"I could go have an extra riding lesson. Everyone could watch me."

Why they all laughed at this I will never understand. I went up the stairs. When I got to my room, I looked out the window. The garden was empty of people but full of flowers. I thought they should go out there. I also thought that maybe Gran and Pop had stayed a little too long. Dad needed to go sell some vacuum cleaners, and Grandma and Grandpa needed to come help Mom with Joan Ariel. Now that Gran and Pop were visiting, there were just too many people in the house, which was probably why Grandma was making herself scarce, as she would say.

I sat on my bed and picked up my book, but then I closed my eyes and let my head fall back, and I made up a story about Ned and me. I was sitting on him bareback, the way I had in the spring, in the round corral, when Abby was inside and no one was looking, and I didn't have a bridle, either, but we were walking along (*sauntering* along), going here and there, looking at things. The whole time, we were talking. I would say, "What's that?" and Ned would say, "That's an eagle. That's a crow. That's a porcupine." And then I would see those animals in my mind, like pictures in a book. The road we walked along was a path, nice and flat and beige. It went up a hill, and then into some birch woods and then out of the woods into a green valley and then up the side of a mountain. In the valley, we stopped, and I sat on Ned while he grazed the green green grass, always saying, "Oh, so delicious! The best grass I ever ate!" and then he wandered to the edge of some woods, and I did something I did once with Abby—I picked blackberries off some branches and ate them. And then, of course, because I am an exaggerator, I also picked raspberries, apples, pears, and even strawberries, because the bushes, I imagined, were on a little cliff beside the path. After we were full, we walked back into the valley, and I said to Ned, "Canter!" and he went up into the most perfect canter in the history of the world, and all I had to do was take one deep breath after another and sit easy on his back.

"Ellen! Are you sleeping?"

My eyes popped open. It was Dad. I said the easiest thing, which was, "Yes."

"I bet you stayed up late last night." He smiled.

I didn't answer. He said, "That's okay. Some people are just night owls. But we're going down the coast. Do you want to come? Mom and Joan Ariel are staying home."

I have never seen a single horse down the coast. It is all boats and cliffs and sometimes a whale. I said, "I'll stay home." And I did.

One more thing happened before Gran and Pop left three days later, and that was that Grandma said she'd come down with something—she didn't have any idea what it was, but it came on quick and so was probably very contagious—and didn't dare give them dinner, the way she had planned. So Gran and Pop didn't get a chance to say good-bye to Grandma and Grandpa, and instead we went to a famous restaurant out near the stables where Blue is, and we all, including Joan Ariel and including me, behaved ourselves. The next day, after a cab came to take Gran and Pop to the airport, everyone relaxed.

Chapter 3

The next Saturday was the thirtieth of September, which made me happy because October would begin the very next day. October is my favorite month, and it is not because my birthday is in October (my birthday is in July), it is because where we live, October has the best weather. The days may be a little short, but the sky is clear, there are boats drifting across the bay, the water in the bay seems extra blue, and there are a lot of flowers that decide to bloom one last time before winter settles in. It's the best time of the year for going to the stables, because the horse shows are over and the golf and the tennis and everything else. It is very quiet.

Which was a good thing, because Abby had a plan, and it was something I'd never done before, and I am not talking about jumping four and a half feet. When I got there—right on time—the late-morning sunlight was sparkling in the trees and my saddle was hanging on the fence of the arena. Blue was in the arena, but wearing Melinda's saddle. Melinda is a little older than I am, but much more nervous. She was standing on the mounting block. She waved to me. Then Sophia came out of the barn leading Onyx, and then Abby leading Gee Whiz, and then Jane leading two horses, Hot Potato and a chestnut, already tacked up. I knew who I was supposed to ride, of course, and I went over to him, pretending to be happy because he is a nice pony and I didn't want him to know what I was thinking. I took the reins from Jane and petted him several times. He didn't seem to notice.

Jane pointed to the saddle, and I led Hot Potato to the railing. Jane said, "I feel like I'm back at summer camp!"

Melinda said, "Are we going to have s'mores when we come back?"

Jane said, "Oh, that's an idea!"

Sophia, who was now sitting on Onyx, who was looking very fondly at the jumps, said, "What are some mores?"

I said, "Roasted marshmallows and chocolate crushed between two graham crackers. Yuck."

Sophia nodded.

After I was mounted, I lined up behind Sophia, probably the safest, but also the most fun, place to be. Jane was in front, Abby on Gee Whiz just behind her, then Melinda, then Sophia, then me. I didn't mind bringing up the rear, because I knew that the pony would want to keep up, and anyway, when you are bringing up the rear, you can watch everyone else.

We went along beside and then behind one of the arenas, and soon we were into the forest. This forest is not like the one I was imagining in the summer, the one I always imagine, with white birch trees and grass, fluttering pale green leaves and plenty of sky; this one is thick and dark—walking into this forest is a little like walking from day into night. The path was wide and sandy, and there was a strong piney odor that smelled like a cross between medicine and fresh air. Hot Potato walked along. I let my legs swing a bit and loosened the reins. Onyx has a beautiful, shiny black hind end. His tail, perfectly brushed, swung back and forth, almost to the ground. I could see a few white hairs in it that I'd never seen before. He is the kind of horse that you don't notice at first, but then he just gets more and more beautiful. I could see Blue, too, though not as well. Melinda was sure to be bridging her reins and holding mane besides and looking here and there for bears and cougars, but Blue would take care of her. He knew his job. In front of him, I saw Gee Whiz. And Gee Whiz did say something—he said, "Let's go!"

Even from all the way in the back, I could see that he was trying to get in front of Jane's horse, and that Abby was tightening her reins and sitting deep. He tossed his head one time. Blue pretended not to notice. Onyx did not notice. Hot Potato might have noticed—I couldn't tell, because he didn't pay any attention. He was watching a blue-and-white bird on a branch that was staring at us, then he looked away. I glanced at Gee Whiz again. Jane's horse walked along, smoothly stepping to the side and stopping Gee Whiz from passing him. Gee Whiz snorted one time, then settled down. The trail began to head downhill. I lowered my heels and leaned back just a little, like everyone else.

At Abby's ranch, the trails lead up into open country. From most of those trails, you can see for a long way—one ridge behind another, blue-green in the spring and golden in the summer and fall. The clouds seem to float in all different, very light shapes, and the sunlight seems to pour down. Here, the sunlight seemed to come through the pine trees in little threads. I could see fine, and so could the horses, since they see better than people do in shadows, but nothing about this trail made me want to trot or canter. This trail seemed to be saying, "Go slow, go slow, go slower." And Hot Potato was listening. I had to kick him a few times to make him keep up with Onyx. Finally, I said, "You have to make an effort." His ears flicked.

Sophia turned and looked at me and said, "Who are you talking to?"

"Hot Potato. I want him to keep up with your horse."

"Oh, I know that. I don't mean that. I mean all that stuff about the trail and the trees and the sunshine."

"Was I talking?"

"You were."

"Sorry."

"Don't be. I was thinking those things, too."

We kept walking and I ran the tip of my forefinger across my lips. That means, "Zip your lip." Sometimes I obey myself.

We walked and walked. For a moment, I imagined

doing this on Ned, let's say bareback and without a bridle, and somehow there would be blackberries, but when I asked Ned, he said, "Never in a million years," and I hoped that was just my imagination talking. There were more birds. There might have been a snake—I only saw it out of the corner of my eye as it was slithering away. I thought how nice it would be to have Rusty along with us, keeping watch. I usually do not think like this, but that is how spooky the forest was. I looked at my watch. Twenty-five minutes since we left the stables.

The trail branched, and then the light in front of us got brighter, and right after that, there we were at exactly the place I should have expected but did not—the ocean, endless and blue with white edges, making its constant noise, and between us and it, a slope through the dunes and the ice plants and the thistles. We moved in a long, careful row, winding between little sandy hills, and then stopped, looked both ways, and crossed the road. Here was the beach itself, pale and flat and dotted with footprints of birds. It was a small cove, not like the big beach near my house, but Jane led us down to the edge of the water.

I said, "Where are we?" And Jane said we were at

the south end of the bay, where the bay meets the Pacific Ocean.

Hot Potato pricked his ears a little, maybe because of the breeze, but I could tell that this, like everything else, was just routine for him. I sat deep, just in case (and I saw Sophia do that, too, though Onyx didn't show any worries). Blue looked around, but Blue always looks around. Then he sighed a couple of times.

It was Gee Whiz who seemed to be saying, as my grandma would, "Oh, heavens to Betsy! What in the world!" Abby was, of course, sitting deep. As soon as Gee Whiz saw (or heard) the waves, he settled back on his heels, pricked his long gray ears, and stared. If his eyes could have been plates, they would have been. Abby hardly even took a tighter grip on the reins (and certainly did not grab mane), though she did give him a little stroke on his shoulder. He had clearly never seen such a thing, not even in his years at the racetrack. We all sat quietly and waited. After three minutes (I checked my watch), he started stepping across the sand, and then Abby walked him along the harder, flatter part of the beach, above the waves. He walked nicely, but he stared, first down, then out, then down, then out again. I laughed, but only to myself. The rest of us walked along, too, but not close to him. Gee Whiz is bossy, and doesn't listen to other horses. One time to the end of the beach, once back the other way to the end of the cove, then to the end of the beach again. Finally, on his own, because I did not see Abby kicking him or even urging him, Gee Whiz stepped toward the waves. When he got into them and they flowed around his hooves, he looked down and his tail lifted. To me, that was the scary bit, because he also snorted, but then he lowered his nose and touched the water, though I didn't see him take a drink. Jane and Sophia now went into the water a little, too, but Melinda was obviously scared, and I preferred watching Gee Whiz. I'm glad I did, because Jane and Sophia did not see what I saw, something I think is the most interesting thing I've ever seen a horse do—he started prancing and playing, splashing, jumping a little bit, splashing again, going into the water up to his knees, then turning and prancing out of it. He stood where it was ankle-deep and did a kind of rhythmic dance, hitting it with the left hoof, then the right, then the left. He kept doing this until Abby was laughing, and then he turned and trotted along the beach, in the water, still prancing and splashing. Hot Potato and I walked behind him. Hot Potato got into the water, too, and was a good boy, but he was just doing a job, not having fun.

When Abby came over to me, I said, "I never saw anything like that before."

"That was a first for me, too."

"What part was the carrot and what part was the stick?"

Abby was quiet for a second, then said, "Only he would know. But he's pretty much the smartest horse I've ever seen. Unless I didn't know what I was seeing."

I said, "He didn't seem afraid. He seemed amazed and then fascinated."

"I thought so, too."

"I wish he would talk to Ned."

Abby sighed. "I think he does talk to Ned, but he only says mean things."

I kept my mouth shut, but I did wonder how she knew.

Hot Potato and I led the walk back to the stables. He was, of course, good. Jane brought up the rear, and Melinda stuck herself firmly between Sophia and Abby, as if that was the safest place, but Blue didn't do one bad thing. The walk back was, like all walks back, much shorter than the walk out, and I mean what I say, even though my watch said a different thing—my watch said it was only a little shorter. When we came out of the forest into the area where the arenas are, Melinda looked like she was about to collapse from exhaustion, so Abby and Jane went to her, and I followed Sophia into the arena and did exactly what she was doing, and if they had asked me, I would have said that that was what I thought I was supposed to do, although I could see our car out of the corner of my eye, and I knew that I was five minutes past my regular lesson time.

Sophia trotted. I trotted. Sophia circled. I circled. Sophia eased up into the canter. I eased up into the canter. Sophia trotted again, then cantered the whole way around the arena. I trotted again, then cantered the whole way around the arena. Now that I'd ridden Blue, I realized that the problem with Hot Potato was that his canter was just bumping along, nothing at all like being inside a dream, the way it was with Blue. Sophia turned and jumped two jumps. I did not turn and jump two jumps. I went back down to the walk and moseyed along, as my grandma would say—still, I have to admit, not noticing either my dad's car or my dad. I kept moseying, Sophia kept jumping, and at last Abby came into the arena. I was caught. I stopped and smiled. You always have to smile when you're not behaving properly.

She ran her hand down Hot Potato's side, then felt the hair between his front legs—that's how you tell whether a horse is heated up or cooled down. She said, "He's cool enough. One more circuit around the arena, then you can put him away. Rodney will untack him, because your dad's here."

I said, "Oh," which is better than saying, "I didn't see him."

I walked around as slowly as I could. There are people, like Abby and Sophia and Jane, who ride every day of the week, or could if they wanted to. I want to be one of those people, but I cannot be. I patted Hot Potato a little along his mane and said, "What do you want to be, Potato? Or, Tater. I will call you Tater, because that's what Dad sometimes says about Mom's mashed potatoes—'Great taters, honey!' So, Tater, what do you want to be?"

He tossed his head to get rid of a fly and didn't answer.

But Dad wasn't in any hurry to get home. The

weather was nice, and he stood there, leaning against the car with his hands in his pockets, facing the forest. I saw him taking some deep breaths, so he must like that pine smell. I said to Rodney when I was dismounting, "Does it always smell like it just got cleaned around here?"

"Aye, you mean that pine scent. Yer mam must use Pine-Sol. I use it meself. Nay, it's the weather and the time of year, especially on a warm day like today. Lovely."

I patted the pony one last time, but I didn't have any treats. He didn't seem to care, walking away without looking. Now Dad came over and said, "Where's Abby? I want to give her this." He pulled a piece of paper out of his pocket—I knew it was a check, for my riding lessons. It was folded up. I took it and said, "I'll give it to her," and ran off before he could stop me. There are kids, most of them boys, who don't know when they're misbehaving, but I do.

Abby was heading for Jane's office, but I held out the check and she stopped. After she took it, while she was putting it in her pocket, I said, "How is Ben?"

"Oh. Ben. Didn't I tell you? He went to a barn down south that specializes in dressage. He's not a bad jumper, but he turned out to have amazing stretch and spring, especially in the trot, so that seemed like a good fit for him."

"What is spring?"

"When the back end is really strong, so it's easier for them to extend. I'll show you pictures sometime. I have a book."

"When did he leave?"

"About a month ago."

"Well," I said, "I think Ned is lonely, and when he stares up the hill, he's looking for a friend."

Abby's eyebrows went up a little bit, and then she cocked her head and patted me on the shoulder. She said, "Maybe. We'll see."

Chapter 4

That afternoon, we took Joan Ariel to Grandma's to have Grandpa's favorite dinner—crab bisque, chicken schnitzel, and cherry pie with vanilla ice cream. It was Grandpa's birthday—sixty-six (he was born in 1901)—and as we walked to their house, I divided the number 66 into all of its parts (33, 2, 3, 11), then I added them up in various ways (44, 5, 6, 2). The numbers seemed to me to be little tiny statues on the lawns we passed. I like numbers.

Joan Ariel got to eat bites of everything, and she opened her mouth like a bird and took it all in, which is not to say that she's good all the time, because most nights she cries for a long time before falling asleep, and some mornings she's very fussy.

After we sang "Happy Birthday," we each asked Grandpa to tell a story from a certain year. I went last. For Dad, Grandpa told a story about his dad buying a Model T Ford, when Grandpa was eleven, for six hundred and fifty dollars. For Mom, Grandpa told about when he turned twenty-five and he spent all the money he'd saved, which was sixty-five dollars, on a brown tweed suit, very flashy, and a pair of brown-and-white wing-tip shoes, all so he could go to a dance where he would see Grandma and chat with her, and she would think he was from New York, or at least LA, but when they got to talking, he realized that she knew he was from our town, and furthermore, she had had her eye on him for ten years. Grandma laughed and said, "That is not true, I did not have my eye on you, but at least I knew that you lived two blocks away and you walked past my house almost every day, even though you never realized it!" And then we laughed. Grandma said, "I still have the dress that I wore to that dance. My aunt sewed it. Someday, all of that will come back into style, I'm sure! Everything looked so beautiful in those days anyway." I asked to see the dress, and she said she would find it sometime.

Grandma asked what Grandpa's very first memory

was, and he swore that it was from when he was Joan Ariel's age, sitting up and staring at his feet, and Grandma said that was impossible, and everyone laughed again, including Joan Ariel. Now it was my turn. Sixty-six divided by four (me, Grandma, Mom, Dad) is sixteen and a half, so I asked for a story from the spring of 1918. Grandpa looked at me for a moment, then said, "Oh, that spring, that wasn't a good spring, and I knew it at the time. Two boys who lived down the street went off to camp because of the war, and they were excited!"

I said, "Which war?"

"The First World War. Have they talked about that in your school yet?"

I shook my head.

"Well, I was too young that spring, but my eyes were open. It wasn't like other wars. I knew it would be bad."

Mom started to shake her head, and Grandma took Joan Ariel into the kitchen. Grandpa sighed, then said, "Well, it turned out I didn't have to go, and one of those boys, George Samuels, he came back okay. The other one, he got gassed because he took off his gas mask at the wrong time. He died."

There was a long silence. I knew I should have picked another year. But then Grandpa said, "Well, darling, you will like this. The previous spring, the spring of 1917, was when Man o' War was born. He was the greatest racehorse of all time, and a tremendous beauty, too. I didn't know it then, nobody did, but that was a good thing to come out of a bad year. Beautiful chestnut."

I said, "There's a book about Man o' War. I saw it at the library, but I haven't checked it out yet."

"I hope it has pictures."

I decided to check it out tomorrow.

Maybe because of all the things we'd talked about, and then because the weather was so bright and sparkly when we were walking home later (and I was imagining Ned walking with us, like a dog), I had a very long and vivid dream that I hope I never forget. I was on the beach, though not at the cove, and other people were behind me, but I didn't turn around to look at them. I was on a horse that looked and acted just like Gee Whiz, but he was a chestnut. I was sitting on him, and he was playing in the waves, and then he began to swim out into the ocean—after a little while, I could feel him swimming underneath me. His head was up, and his ears were pricked, and he was very strong. In the dream, I was not afraid at all. Out in the middle of the bay, two porpoises began swimming around us in a circle, which made me a little dizzy, and this went on so long that I thought we were getting near another beach, the one across the bay.

And then I woke up, and even though I hadn't been afraid in the dream, I was afraid now, so I sat up in bed and I touched the wall and the headboard and the bedside table and the two books on the table, and I stuck my feet out from under the covers and put them on the wood floor, which was chilly and woke me up. Then I went back to sleep, but when I woke up in the morning, I stayed in bed for a while, trying to decide whether it was a bad dream or a good dream. What I decided was that the whole twenty-four hours since going out to the stables for my ride had been so strange that I would be really glad, the next day, to get up and walk to school and be bored for a while.

Later, though, I did walk to the library with Mom and Joan Ariel, and I did check out the Man o' War book, and at bedtime, I was a little sad that no matter how hard I tried to close my eyes and look for Ned so that I could tell him about all the things we had done, he wasn't there.

Monday morning, when I went out our front door, I was looking at my saddle shoes, partly to decide whether they were properly tied, but also because now that Mom had shown me a picture of wing tips, I was imagining having a pair of those. That was why I didn't see Jimmy Murphy walking up the street. That was okay, though, because when you are walking a few steps behind someone, you can spy on him and nobody says a word about it. Jimmy is always late to school and I am always early, which is why I never see him. And usually he is dressed in jeans and a T-shirt. One time, I heard him tell Frankie Crandall that he liked his jeans to be so dirty that he could take them off at night and they would stand up in the corner of his room. When I heard this, I laughed to myself, but maybe it wasn't a joke. Today, he was wearing khaki pants, nice loafers, and a blue shirt. His hair was cut (Mrs. Murphy cuts all the boys' hair herself). He started out walking fast and then he slowed down like he just couldn't help himself, and so I caught up with him. We were almost there. I said, "You look nice."

"But I'm not."

"Excuse me?"

He shook his head, and he had a really sad look on his face.

When we got to the corner, a car went past, and then another. We stood there. Finally, because somebody had to do it, I said, "What's wrong?"

He shook his head again.

And about a moment later, a tear came out of the corner of his eye and rolled down his face. It glinted. I put my hand on his shirt and turned right. I thought we could be late, because I never am and he always is. We started walking. Two times I said, "Tell me," and then at the next corner, he looked at me and said, "What did you do yesterday?"

"We went to the library. What did you do?"

"We spent the day at the hospital."

I knew I had to say this: "Why?"

"Because when everyone was getting dressed for ten o'clock Mass, I got mad at Brian and threw something at him. I didn't mean to hit him, but he moved and the thing hit him and knocked him out. He got a concussion. Do you know what that is?"

I nodded. Everyone who rides horses knows what a concussion is. Then I said, "What did you throw at him?"

He held up our social studies book, which is pretty big because it has maps. I always do my social studies homework at school so I don't have to carry that book back and forth. We were now walking downhill, away from the school. I said, "Is Brian okay?"

Jimmy shrugged. Then he said, *"Mea culpa, mea culpa, mea maxima culpa."*

"What does that mean?"

"My fault. My fault. My biggest fault." He sighed. "I think my family hates me now."

"Do you have to start being good all the time?"

"I think so."

We walked to the bottom of the street and stopped at the corner. I said, "Then we'd better get to school. Between you and me, just keep your eye on Melanie and copycat her. She's always good. She is from the Planet of the Good, and she can't help herself."

Jimmy smiled like this was funny, and we turned

around and walked back up the street. We were ten minutes late. I went in first, walked over to Mr. Nathan, apologized for being late, smiled, and went to my desk. Jimmy did what I did, instead of just scooting to his desk, sitting down, and grinning the way he usually does. Mr. Nathan gave him one of those "Are you kidding me?" looks, and then we continued with the morning work, which was spelling. I like spelling. I like that "toe" and "though" rhyme with "blow," but "plow" doesn't.

And Jimmy Murphy kept to himself all day, even at lunch and at recess after lunch. The other boys might have teased him, but they didn't dare, I guess. After school got out, I saw him go in the door of the school library. Of course I went straight home and found my mom and asked her, "Do you know what happened to Brian Murphy?"

She was sitting in the easy chair by the window in the living room, the window that looks across the street, and for sure, since both the window and the door were closed, no Murphy could hear her, but she lowered her voice anyway and said, "They think he'll be all right. That just happens with little kids, they fall down and hit their heads. Just happens." She gave Joan Ariel a kiss on the forehead. "So many children! It's a wonder nothing's happened before this."

I said, "Remember last winter, when Brian liked to sit by the curb and put leaves and sticks in puddles and watch them float down the hill?"

"I saw that one time."

"He did it all the time."

"That's just what I'm saying." She put her arm around me and gave me a little squeeze. I said, "What made him fall down?"

"No one knows. Must have been running around and slipped. Teresa does her best, but that house is a mess."

I didn't say anything and went upstairs to change out of my school clothes.

I didn't think much about Jimmy Murphy after that until I was walking through the living room to get an oatmeal cookie, as my reward for answering all of my division problems correctly, and heard Dad talking about how he missed one of his favorite TV shows. Mom watched it sometimes with him, but it isn't on anymore. The name of the show was, I am not kidding, *I've Got a Secret*. This show came on on Monday nights, and Dad had been watching it my whole life.

That word "secret" got stuck in my head: "I've got a secret. I've got a secret." I went into the kitchen and stood over the cookie jar. When I lifted the lid, I said, "Secret, I am leaving you in this jar," and then I took out my cookie and put the lid on so that it fit perfectly. I went into the living room. Dad was watching another show, tapping his fingers and nodding his head from side to side in time with the music. Dad loves music. In the closet of his and Mom's room there is a black case with a trumpet in it. He never plays it, but he used to. I listened to the man play the song, which afterward they said was "Here We Go Again," and I let that song push my secret, a real secret, out of my head. I did that again before I fell asleep, and again in the morning when I saw Jimmy Murphy across the classroom, still being good, this time dressed in a white shirt. And I did it again when I was walking home and saw Jane Murphy and Brian sitting on their porch steps.

Chapter 5

It is exhausting to keep a secret when half the time you don't even know whether you're talking or not. I would have said that my conversations with Ned were a secret, but maybe not, maybe I did talk about them, and maybe everyone thought that I was just telling a story. And maybe I was. I was beginning to think that I had told this story all spring, and now that story was over. This made me sad, especially since the Tater story wasn't as good as the Ned story. Tater is a nice pony and such a strange color that everyone looks at him. I knew that if I went to a horse show on Tater, he would go around all the jumps, and people would give me lots of compliments, and my dad would take pictures, and it would be a dream come true, but so far, it didn't feel like a dream come true, because riding Tater was like driving a car—turn it on, go somewhere, turn it off, forget about it.

Anyway, until Thursday, I paid attention to whether I was saying anything at all about Jimmy Murphy—at home, at school, at recess, at lunch, looking out the window, looking out the door, when Mom was around, when Dad was around. I'm sure that some people, maybe even Melanie, would have said that I should tell Jimmy's secret, but I thought that it wasn't my business. If I wanted to tell his secret, then I should have gone to him and told him that I was going to. But he stayed away from me—no spitballs, no jokes written on bits of paper and passed around behind Mr. Nathan's back, no making faces in class, no getting together with the other bad boys in the corner of the playground and planning something. And then on Thursday, at lunch, right after I asked Melanie if she was still taking ballet, and she was telling me that she had moved on to something called modern dance, where you could be taller and you didn't have to wear a tutu, I glanced at Ruthie Creighton, who was eating a salami sandwich and had an orange sitting on her paper bag and was saying nothing. I realized that maybe Ruthie wasn't quiet; maybe she was an expert keeper of secrets, like a combination safe or a lock box. If that was true, then it was for sure that all her secrets weren't bad—they were just secrets—and maybe, like me, she wanted to tell some of them but didn't dare.

After lunch, we went outside. It was a nice day. Ruthie and I followed Melanie to the hopscotch area and we started to play. Melanie is so good at this that if you play with her, your job is to stand around while she goes all the way, because your turns are few and far between. Melanie even has a piece of chalk that she uses to extend the hopscotch grid so that it will be more challenging. Really, there should be a hopscotch Olympics for girls like Melanie, but there isn't. When she got to 7–8, I said, "Show us a modern dance move," and so she hopped into 7, kicked up, and did a split, picking up her pebble from 8 before her leg touched the ground, then somehow launched herself so that she landed standing on both feet in the 8. Ruthie and I then closed our mouths and stopped nodding and gave her a round of applause. I said, "You should be in a circus. You could gallop everywhere standing up on the back of a horse and do somersaults and handstands."

Melanie said, "I'm afraid of horses."

I said, "You must be joking."

Melanie said, in her quiet, calm way, "I'm not."

And Ruthie said, "Do you really have a horse?"

I said, "No, I wish I did. But I take a lesson every weekend."

She went on. I kept my mouth closed as if this weren't a one-time event. She said, "I saw that book you have, about Man o' War."

"I've got it for another ten days. You can borrow it from me, and then I'll take it back."

She gave me a long long look and said, "Okay."

And I said, "Do you want to come with me to the barn? You don't have to ride, but you can see the horses."

She started shaking her head no, and then she stopped, and then she said, "Yes." And then she smiled. And then Melanie and I smiled, too. We just couldn't help it.

I told my dad—he didn't care. It only takes fifteen minutes to get to the stables from our house, and Ruthie's house is on the way. On Saturday, she was waiting at the bottom of the stairs with her aunt, who was smiling. I got out of the car and gave her the once-over, as my grandma would say, and then I said that she had to wear heavier shoes, and then there was a long silence, and I realized that she didn't have any other shoes, and her aunt laughed and said, "Oh, when I was a child, we ordered our shoes from a catalog, and we wore them for a year whether they fit or not," and Dad said, "Me too!" Everyone was smiling, and we got into the car. Ruthie was quiet all the way there, and I was quiet because Dad had the radio on and he was humming to the music.

I took Ruthie into the barn, where Rodney was standing with the tack. He was talking to Abby about something. He shook my hand and bowed, and then he said, "And who might this young lady be?"

I said, "This is Ruthie, she wants to watch," and her hand went out on its own and got near Tater's neck, and then she pulled it back, but I started petting Tater, and I said, "Tater likes to be petted," and I showed her how. Because Rodney is such a good groom, petting Tater's neck is like running your hand across the surface of a quiet lake.

Abby said, "Tater is a good name. I don't like it when a horse has 'hot' in his name. He might take the hint."

I said to Ruthie, "'Hot' means 'hard to handle.'"

Ruthie pulled her hand back, but I kept petting him, and after a moment, she petted him again.

I led him out of the barn and over to the schooling arena. There was another kid in there. I went to the mounting block and got on. Abby showed Ruthie where to stand, under a tree by the fence, and then the breeze came up and I forgot about Ruthie, and, really, about every single thing except this lesson, which I'd been waiting for all week.

Tater *sauntered* into the ring on a loose rein, looked toward the forest, then toward a couple of jumps. I went into one corner while the other kid, who was being taught by Colonel Hawkins, finished his course. The colonel has such a loud voice that it makes you wince every time he shouts a command, but his students win a lot of ribbons and they do something called combined training, which includes galloping around a jumping course that is not in a ring and also doing some jumping in the woods. I don't know much about it, but probably it's not as scary as the sound of the colonel's voice.

Now Abby came into the ring and the other kid and the colonel went out. I watched them go to a warm-up arena, where the kid got off and the colonel walked with him, talking the whole time. I guess the colonel doesn't have any secrets, either. I asked Tater to trot. Which he did. "Yeah, okay, don't hold me so tight, there's a fly in my nose [*snort*], okay, I will speed up [*sigh*]." Abby was smiling. I was talking. I pressed my lips together, and Abby said, "See that *A* on the fence? Go there, then trot to the *B* and the *C* and the *E*." We'd done this before—it was a diamond, and is for practicing turns. "At *C*, halt and ask Tater to turn by stepping under." I made a little turn at the *B*, then trotted (nicely, I thought) to the *C*, where I sat deep and Tater halted, and why wouldn't he, since otherwise he would run into the railing? Now I lifted my left rein, which lifted his nose and cocked his neck, and we stood there for what seemed like a long time, and then he did step under and we were pointed toward the *E*. I kicked him and he trotted toward the *E*, then back to the *A*. One good thing was that there weren't any jumps in the way, and we could go in straight lines. Abby said, "Again! This time, push him into the turns so that he has some energy and wants to get out of them." I did the exercise two more times to the left, then twice to the right. I would have expected it to be boring, but it wasn't, and it warmed up Tater, so that he was actually pricking his ears and holding the bit in his mouth without pulling on it. After that, we cantered twice around the arena in each direction and then did two figure eights at the canter, and yes, Tater does an excellent flying change, which means that when he crosses the center of the figure eight, he seems to hop a little bit, and then he is on the other lead. A horse is supposed to lead with his left foot when he is circling to the left and the right foot when he is circling to the right. Abby said, "Maybe it's easier for a pony to change leads. I never thought of that." I pressed my lips closed again and came down to the walk. Now I remembered Ruthie and looked over to the tree where she was standing. She was still standing there, but her sweater was partly unbuttoned and her hair was in her face. I went over to her but didn't say anything except, "You could pet him now. That would let him know he's being good." I stood Tater beside the fence and started petting him. Ruthie did come over. She tried to reach through the fence. That didn't work, so she climbed the fence and leaned over. She put her hand under his mane. She smiled. I wanted her to say that she would like to ride him, but she didn't. When I walked away, she stayed on the fence.

Now the jumping. Abby set me two courses, eight jumps each, just like in a show. The first one was around the arena to the left, a crossbar into the far corner from the barn, then down over three jumps, one single and one an in-and-out, then to the right, a loop over a small chicken coop, stay to the right, then out of the corner over a small oxer, then turn slightly right, two more, one of them a panel, then turn left and make a small circle, come down to the trot, the walk, the halt. I took a deep breath, patted Tater on the neck, loosened the reins. I glanced over at Ruthie. She was still standing on the fence rail, staring now. Maybe she didn't know about jumping. Abby waved. I went over to her and she set me another course, some of the same jumps, but going the other way. She talked, I nodded. She said, "You got it?" I nodded. I turned Tater to the right, trotted a little circle, pushed him up into the canter, rode the course. Was I doing it right? I had no idea, but it seemed right. After the last jump (the coop), I circled, came down to the trot, to the walk. Leaned forward, wrapped my right hand loosely around Tater's thick white-and-red mane, pulled my hand gently toward myself, and said, "Good boy."

Abby put her hand on my leg and said, "Really good."

Which meant, I guess, that I had done my course correctly, and how I managed that I will never know. I guess there is a way that directions just go into you, and you follow them.

I walked Tater twice around the arena, and then it was time for someone else to take a lesson from the colonel, so I went out the gate and jumped off Tater. Rodney was standing there. He waited until I had undone all the buckles, as if I were the one untacking Tater, but then he grinned and thanked me, put Tater's halter on, and took the tack. I led Tater over to where Ruthie still was, because she always does what she is told to do, and I said, "Let's walk him. I'll teach you how." She looked a little scared, but Tater is just a pony. Sometimes I'm lazy about walking Tater the right way, but this time I did it—by his head, on his left, the lead rope in my right hand, my hand about a foot from the buckle, the rest of the lead rope crossing me in front so that I could hold it in my left hand, no loops, not dragging on the ground, step step step. Ruthie walked beside me. After seven minutes, I didn't even ask her if she wanted to try it—I just stopped, handed her the lead rope in the right way, and went to her left side. After a moment, she started walking. Tater was good. Ruthie kept looking at him, and I told her that he was a red roan Welsh cob, and you never see one of those. She said, "I think he's beautiful."

That was the first thing she'd said all morning.

When Dad got there (we had to wait a little while), he had a bag, and in the bag were two blueberry muffins and two napkins. That made me pretty quiet on the way home, because I love blueberry muffins.

You can always tell when you have left the town that the stables are in and come into our town, because the houses go instantly from being huge, on big lots, to being small, on tiny lots. I was just eating the last bite of my muffin when I noticed this, and Ruthie must have noticed it, too, because she said, "We're moving."

My dad said, "Where to?"

I said, "When?"

But she didn't answer either of these questions.

Chapter 6

The ickiest thing that happened on Monday was that after school, I happened to walk out the front entrance with Todd, who was telling me about going to the beach boardwalk in the summer, they were there for four days, they went on every ride twenty-seven times, but then he stopped talking and I looked at him, only to see him bend down and pick up a piece of bubble gum, mutter to himself, "Finders keepers, losers weepers," and then pop it in his mouth. I didn't say anything, but I walked faster, because I hoped that he would get distracted by something and not follow me home. Even though you don't pass my house to get to his, sometimes he follows me to mine and then stands there waiting for an oatmeal cookie, which Mom gives him just to get rid of him. But—good luck—Paulie Miller came running up to us and started talking to Todd about the Cardinals and the World Series and Bob Gibson, who is a pitcher, and so I got away from them. The only time I like baseball is in the spring, when we play a little softball during recess and some-times I hit the ball, which is a good feeling.

At our house, everything was extra quiet, which meant, I am sorry to say, that I might as well do my arithmetic problems, because I had finished *Man o' War* and given it to Ruthie that morning. I ate the cookie that Mom had left for me, saw that her door was closed, which meant that she was taking a nap along with Joan Ariel, and went up to my room and closed my door. If Mom had been there, I'm sure I would have told her that Todd had eaten raw liver and onions off the street, but she wasn't, so I didn't. First I drew two pictures of Ned, then two pictures of Tater, and I tried very hard to make them not look alike, be-cause they don't look alike. Even if their heads were the same color, they would not look alike. While I was dividing 492 by 24 (20, remainder 12), Joan Ariel woke up crying, and then Mom started talking, and then, step step step (creak creak creak, because our house is old), they went into the kitchen, and the crying stopped. Joan Ariel is six months old now. I like her. When she first wakes up in the morning or from a nap, she screams "to wake the dead," as Grandma says, but she stops as soon as she gets picked up. She knows what she wants, which is a good thing. I am sure she will want a horse someday, because when I show her horse pictures, she points at them and smiles. She's a really good smiler, which is probably why I like her so much. She also has plenty of hair now. It's lighter brown than mine, and a little wavy, not like mine, which is long and straight, has always been straight, according to Mom. Melanie has wavy hair, and if she wants it to look nice, she just shakes it with her fingers and it sort of flops around her head in just the right way.

I finished my division problems and went downstairs. Mom was walking across the living room with Joan Ariel on her shoulder, patting her back. When I stepped off the bottom step, there was a burp. Mom smiled and said, "Like magic!" Then she put Joan Ariel in the corner of the sofa, propped against the arm and the back, and I sat down and played some games with her—patty-cake, hide-and-seek, peekaboo, and a game I made up where I use my legs as drums and my hands as sticks, and I play her tunes like "When the Saints Go Marching In." It was fun. *She* is fun. When I look at her, I think that before she came along, our house was *way* too quiet.

At dinner, even though I'd been thinking about it all day, I said only one thing: "I wonder where Ruthie is moving."

Dad said, "Don't you."

Mom said, "No idea."

Joan Ariel said, "Ah ah ah," just like she was offering her opinion, and we all laughed.

By Thursday, we knew. Here's how it happened:

Grandpa went to the market. The two men in front of him in line were complaining. One of them said, "Breaking the lease, too, I'll be bound." The other one said, "Shouldn't have given them a lease in the first place. Even when the husband was around, they were late with the rent, is what I heard."

The woman behind the counter said, "Shame on you, talking like that. They used to go to my church. They had their troubles."

The two men walked out, and Grandpa put his

groceries on the counter. He said, "Everyone has their troubles."

"Some more than others. Since my pa didn't die of the TB when I was fourteen, leaving me to take care of my family, I try not to complain."

Grandpa told this to Grandma over dinner.

Grandma said, "Oh, that was Isaac Creighton who died." That was Ruthie's grandfather.

Grandpa said, "Don't remember the son's name."

The next day, Grandma was talking to a woman in her knitting group. She said, "You remember Isaac Creighton, Lorena."

"I do. He was the quietest boy you ever saw. But then he died. I remember every time he opened his mouth, he would cover it with his handkerchief and cough." Grandma said, "What was his son's name?" Lorena said, "Albert. He married Frances Cannon. Another quiet one. Who knows what in the world those two ever talked about. Then he took some money from the cannery. Disappeared." And Grandma said, "Everyone knows. Less said about that, the better." And Lorena said, "I hate gossip. I never gossip." And so they had to stop talking about it.

The next day, Grandma and Mom had Joan Ariel down at the department store, and they saw Ruthie's mom and aunt, Frances and Nancy, walking past the window. The window is very long, so they watched them for a long time. The lady behind them said, "They do their best." Then she shook her head.

Mom said, "Do you know them?"

"They live two doors down from me."

Now Mom and Grandma waited, which, I am here to tell you, is what you've got to do when you want to find out something.

They waited until the lady looked at all of the towels, then smelled all of the soaps, then everyone watched Ruthie's mom and aunt cross the street, and the lady said, "Well, they can't afford it here anymore. They don't say where they are going. I heard they found someplace for half the rent. I hope they can afford that, is all I can say."

Then everyone shook their heads, and, Mom told me at dinner, no one bought anything, which is what happens if you are in the department store and you start to feel bad. Mom worked there for a long time, so she knows.

The way it came up was that when we were eating

our dinner, she said, "I'm sorry there's no dessert. I was going to buy some apple tarts, but I got so down when I was shopping that I just came home and forgot about it."

Dad was still away selling vacuum cleaners, so I said, "Why did you get down?" I imagined her climbing down a ladder. That was when she told me about the gossip trail that led to us knowing about Ruthie. I said, "When do you think she's going to move?"

Mom shrugged. "I guess you'll know when she disappears from school." She sat back in her chair and looked around the dining room, then out the window at her garden. She still seemed down. I didn't know why. Right then, Joan Ariel started to cry. I cleared the table without being asked. And because I didn't want to think about Ruthie, I imagined all the horses at Abby's place gossiping about Ned. "He's just young," said Sissy. "We were all young once." (Grandma says this.) "I knew horses like him at the racetrack," said Gee Whiz. "Scared of their own shadows. Wouldn't leave the pack and actually win a race." He snorted. "His pa was like that," said another horse that I imagined and named Ralph. "That kind of thing runs in the family." "You got to have a decent job that you love," said Beebop, who then ran leaping and kicking across the pasture, and all the horses got out of the way. I saw Ned so clearly in the distance looking at the others, taking a bite of hay, looking up the hill, pricking his ears. But he said nothing.

Sometimes, when I lie in bed at night, wide awake, and lots of times I am wide awake, I wonder why being ten is so much different from being nine. Six months ago, I was nine. Six months doesn't seem all that long (but ask Joan Ariel—six months is her whole lifetime), but when I remember being nine, all I remember is doing what I wanted to do, or at least keeping at wanting it until I was finally allowed to do it. There is this book that Mom used to read to me, back before I could read for myself, called *The Little Engine That Could*. The engine in the book has a face, and it has to pull a train full of toys up a mountain. Your job, if your mom is reading it to you, is to say to yourself, "I think I can, I think I can." I remember that even when Mom wasn't reading it to me, I would turn the pages and look at the animals in the train cars, and maybe "I think I can" were the first words that I learned to read. It seems like I've been saying that ever since then. I was sure that the only good thing about growing up would be that I would get to do what I wanted every day, all the time. I didn't really understand about things like Ruthie's grandpa dying when her dad was fourteen, and her dad having to go to work to support his mom. (I have been to the cannery—that's where they used to bring the fish from the bay and put them in cans and send them out to be sold. It is run-down and a little scary, though my dad loves sardines.) My great-aunt died, too, and that's how we got this house—she left it to my mom in her will because Grandpa and Grandma had their own house, which is bigger and has a bigger yard. I've always known that she was forty-five when she died, but either I never thought about forty-five until I got to be ten, or I never cared, but now I think that forty-five is pretty young—only four and a half times ten. Mom and Dad and Grandma and Grandpa never talk about her, except to say what a wonderful gardener she was and how, if it weren't for her, our garden would just be a few roses and tulips and dandelions. But was gardening what she wanted to do? I don't know.

What we do at school is different now, too. In fourth grade, Miss Cranfield just wanted right answers. She would ask a question, and if you cared, you would raise your hand. Melanie had the right answers 100 percent of the time, I had the right answers 95 percent of the time, and Jimmy Murphy never raised his hand. One of the boys, Brodie Maxwell, just sat at his desk and picked his nose. I am not saying where he put it, but finders keepers, losers weepers. I know which desk was his (it had the initials *LP* scraped into one corner by someone long ago, and the school never sanded them away). I wouldn't go near that desk. If Miss Cranfield called out, "Brodie, what do you think?" he would jerk in his chair like she'd startled him to death and his mouth would drop open, but he never had an answer. The other kids lots of times had some right answers and some wrong answers, but we all acted like it didn't matter much—what mattered was passing notes and making faces and avoiding spitballs. (Though one time, which made me laugh out loud, so that Miss Cranfield's head whipped around to see what I was laughing at, Brad Caswell looked at Jimmy Murphy and opened his mouth wide, and Jimmy Murphy threw a spitball across three desks and two rows and made the basket. I wasn't the only one laughing, either.) In fifth grade, we still answer questions, but Mr. Nathan likes to have discussions. That social studies book Jimmy Murphy hit Brian with is really big because it is full of discussions—first there's a story with some pictures, then a couple of lists, then some questions. And yes, I still have my hand up all the time, because I always have something to say, but then other kids have something to say, and I don't always end up agreeing with myself. You could say that school is more interesting now, but I'm not sure that's good.

Later that night I started thinking about Tater, not Ned. My lesson on Tater was getting closer and closer. There he was, red, white, cute. He is much more cooperative than the pony I rode before I started riding Blue. He's perfectly trained, and you don't have to worry about anything when you're on him. I'm sure he will be great in a show, if I get to go in a show next spring (I'm not stupid—I started saving some of my own money for that in the summer, and I now have four dollars and eighty-five cents); we could have ribbons coming out of our ears. But as I lay in bed staring at the ceiling, I thought, "Ho hum, turn left, turn right, go around in a circle, jump the coop. Bleh."

And then I thought that what was really going on was that there were so many things to think about— Tater, Ruthie, Ned, Aunt Johanna, Jimmy Murphy, the Pilgrims, the cannery, Joan Ariel, the path through the forest, Mr. Nathan asking questions all the time with his pencil tapping on his teeth and his eyebrows up by his hair—that for the first time in my life, I didn't know what to think. So I closed my eyes, stopped looking at the quarter-moon out my window (the moon is always brightest in the fall), and I thought, "Ned! Ned!" There he was, off in the distance, but he didn't come closer. One thing did happen, though—I heard Abby's dad singing that song, "From this valley they say you are going. We will miss your bright eyes and sweet smile," and I let that song go around my head all night long, and it was still there when I woke up in the morning. I hummed it over breakfast, and Mom gave me such a nice, happy look. She said, "I've always loved that song."

Chapter 7

On Friday, Ruthie did pass me the Man o' War book back at lunch. During reading time, I read a little of it again. When I walked home, I was in a pretty good mood, even though it was not sunny and I could barely see the bay. I hummed. Everything was quiet in the house. I kissed Mom. Joan Ariel was still napping. I ate my cookie going up the stairs, then I spent some time copying the picture on the front cover. Man o' War was a chestnut, all red everywhere. Very flashy, as Grandma would say, and then roll her eyes.

Things stayed quiet. No crying. Not even much noise out on the street. And then Dad was late for dinner because he'd gotten a flat tire on the way home.

While Mom was pulling the fried chicken out of

the oven and shaking her head, Dad said, "Don't worry about it, I like it crisp!" Then he said, "Ellen, after dinner, let's call Oak Valley Ranch and see if you can have your lesson out there tomorrow." Oak Valley Ranch is the name of Abby's place. He was quite jolly for someone who'd had to change his tire and been an hour and a half late for dinner. Usually, Dad likes his dinner right on time. Joan Ariel was sitting in her high chair. He took her out and bounced her on his knee. She started waving her arms.

By the time he called Abby, it was after nine. Abby gets up really early, so I thought she might have already gone to bed, but I didn't say anything. I could hear them talking and talking and talking.

He knocked on my door and pushed it open. I was reading my chapter of *The Witch of Blackbird Pond* for reading class. He still seemed very happy. He said, "Okay! She can't do the lesson until three, and Tater is at the stables, so you have to ride Sissy."

I said, "At least Sissy has some personality."

Dad laughed and kissed me good night.

In the morning, it was misting, but I didn't have a thing to do, so I walked with Mom to the market and helped her choose apples for apple tarts. And for Ned.

Everything about that Saturday was strange. We left early, so that Dad dropped me at the ranch before two. It was misting there, too. He then pulled out of the driveway and drove off with a wave. Abby and her mom were gone, so I had to be with Mr. Lovitt all by myself. The first thing I did was walk over to the pasture fence and call out to Ned, but I didn't need to—he and Gee Whiz came trotting over like they were old friends, and yes, Gee Whiz pushed Ned's nose out of the way for the first piece of apple, but he did let Ned have the second piece. And the third. But then, when I was talking to Ned ("Hi, Ned, do you miss me, how are you?"), Gee Whiz tossed his head and trotted off and Ned followed him, and about six times I had to remind myself that maybe I was not his best friend. I went over to the mare fence. Sissy was standing there, so I gave her a piece of apple, too. The mist had stopped and everything smelled nice, so I went and sat on Abby's back porch and watched Rusty dig a hole for a while until Mr. Lovitt came out of the barn and chased her away and kicked the dirt back into the hole and stamped on it. He smiled at me, took off his cowboy hat, shook his head, put his hat back on, and looked at his watch. I said, "What song were you just humming?"

He sniffed, then said, "Well, I have to think about it."

"'Red River Valley'?"

"Maybe. I have a song running through my head all the time." Then he scratched his chin and said, "Oh, I remember, 'Lorena.'" And he started singing, "The years creep slowly by, Lorena, the snow is on the grass again. The sun's low down the sky, Lorena, the frost gleams where the flowers have been."

We were outside, but the tune rose anyway, like it was vibrating on the still air and wrapping around me. I must have smiled, because he smiled, too, and went on, "A hundred months have passed, Lorena, since last I held that hand in mine." The tune seemed to expand. I saw why he had such a beautiful voice—his mouth was really big, and he didn't mind opening it all the way. After another verse, he said, "I'll stop. It's a very long song."

"I never heard that one before."

"It's old. From before the Civil War."

"The Civil War was a hundred years ago. It's in our social studies book."

"I'm sure it is. Well, Abby should be home soon. You want to start grooming Sissy?"

I said I did, and so he got her out of the pasture for

me, and we walked along to the barn just like he was not the scariest man I know. Then he handed me the brushes, and while I was grooming her, he sang the song again while he was cleaning stalls, this time in a low voice, like he couldn't help himself, but because I have excellent hearing, I sang along in my own mind and made the words with my lips, which is a good way to memorize something. I didn't mind that Abby was late (3:10), because it was fine sitting on Sissy while she wandered around the arena, making her go, but letting her go where she wanted, and also watching Ned from a distance. He looked a little ragged, the way horses do in autumn, when their summer coats are falling out and their winter coats are growing in. When I petted Sissy, some of her hair, in short clumps, came into my hand. The hair that was growing in was darker than the hair that was falling out, and it was smooth and made me want to pet her more. Sissy was turning into a good horse. I should have wanted Sissy.

Abby still had her raincoat on when she opened the gate. She took it off, wedged it between the gate and the fence, then said, "Half an inch! Not here, I know, but at the stables. It could come this way if we're lucky. Okay, hi, how are you? She looks good!" And so I let the song go out of my brain, but I knew it would come back if I wanted it to.

Sissy is not a Thoroughbred, like Ned. She is half quarter horse and half whatever, as Abby's dad once said, something old-fashioned like a driving horse, because she will trot faster and faster in order to avoid cantering, so you have to ask her to canter from the walk. Once she is cantering, she doesn't mind continuing to canter. Abby said, "Transitions! Transitions! We're going to do a *lot* of transitions," and we did. A lot of transitions means you have to pay attention, and so I couldn't keep my eye on Ned in the pasture anymore. Which was a good thing, because I could stop thinking about him turning and following Gee Whiz when he trotted away from the fence.

We did the transitions by the numbers—eight walking steps, then trot. Eight strides at the trot, then walk. Two walking steps, then do your best to get her to canter. Okay, three walking steps, try again. Across the diagonal, step step step, right in the center, ask for the canter. This one I did just right, and it felt good, too—Sissy lifting herself up and rocking forward. After that, Abby let me canter one whole circuit to the right, and then it was back to transitions. Sissy was saying, "Oh, my goodness me, so complicated!" She sounded just like my grandma. Now serpentine transitions. Start at the far end of the arena, curve through the jumps, first left, then right. In the middle of every curve, transition up or down, walk-trot, trot-walk, walk-canter, canter-halt, halt-trot, trot-walk, walk-halt. Now the hard one, halt-canter. Hooray, no problem. Abby came running over, patted me on the leg, and gave Sissy a lump of sugar. The more transitions we did, the better Sissy did them. I must have been talking about this without realizing it, because Abby said, "Yes, it's partly that her muscles loosen up, but it's also that her mind loosens up. She gets into the habit of paying attention."

I said, "Oh." Then, "How long have I been talking?"

"Five minutes or so."

"What else did I say?"

"Well, you sang a song."

"Your dad taught me a song." I sang the first line of "Lorena."

She said, "My dad has a cousin—well, second cousin—who plays guitar and sings. He's in a band called Mad Hatter."

"That's from *Alice in Wonderland*."

"Ellen, have you read everything?"

"Not yet." I was serious, but Abby laughed anyway. We continued with transitions, adding in some jumping exercises. The first one was to do a figure eight—transition to the canter at the end of the arena, go down the diagonal on the left lead, jump the two (small) jumps on that line, halt at the other end of the arena, canter off on the right lead, and take two more jumps down the right diagonal. I said, "Do I change leads?"

"No, let her choose. See what she chooses."

Sissy is much better trained than she was, because after the second jump on the left lead, she saw where she was headed and landed on her right lead. After that, she was a little slow halting, but she did it better on the second try. I had my lips pressed closed so that I would not say anything. I was not actually afraid that I would tell Jimmy Murphy's secret to Abby—she doesn't know who in the world Jimmy Murphy is—but practice makes perfect, as Mom would (does) say.

Now we did something more complicated. You can't stop your horse when she's facing the jump, or she will think that you want her to refuse, so I went over a jump in the middle of the arena, turned right, cantered a circle, went past the jump to the rail, came down to the walk, turned in a little circle, then cantered to the left and down over the jump going the other way, doing the whole thing backward. It was hard to remember, and took me three times, but at least Abby wasn't screaming commands the way the colonel does at the stables. When I was done and walking around, I walked past Abby, and she said, "It's okay to talk. You can talk." I nodded, but didn't say anything. I cooled Sissy out and looked for Ned. He was at the far end of the pasture, in the shade of some trees. Their leaves fluttered a little in the late-afternoon breeze. I thought his name, I whispered his name, I thought his name again, with my eyes closed. I opened my eyes. He hadn't moved. It was now four, but no Dad. Dad is getting more and more peculiar.

When Sissy was untacked and put away, Dad still hadn't shown up, so Abby said, "Let's put Ned in the round corral for a few minutes."

I said, "Let's teach him a trick."

"Let's do!"

Blue knows tricks, but no one has ever taught Ned a trick.

By the time we got to the gate of the pasture, the

horses must have thought it was suppertime, because they were all standing there. Abby let me lead Ned from the pasture to the round corral. He wasn't terribly good—he trotted a couple of strides and got in front of me, but I slowed down like molasses, and he stopped trotting and turned to look at me. We went into the round corral. Abby came over to where I was standing outside the railing and showed me her pocket. Sugar lumps.

But the first thing Ned had to do was walk and trot in both directions, to loosen up, which he did, only once turning his head and then tossing it when someone in the pasture whinnied—maybe Gee Whiz, but not as loud as I remembered Gee Whiz being. Ned knows how to be good. Finally, Abby backed up a step and lowered the whip, and Ned looped and trotted toward her. He stopped. She said, "Good boy," and stroked his cheek. She crooked her finger. I climbed through the bars and went to the middle. She whispered, "What trick?"

I whispered, "Telling left from right."

"That's a useful one!"

Ned was staring at us with his ears pricked, like he was eavesdropping. This is how we did it. I took his halter and led him to the middle of the round corral, then stood beside him. Abby stood behind him, maybe five feet away. Then she lifted her left arm to the side and said, "Ned! Go left!" I gently moved his head to the left and clucked. After a moment, he turned and walked to the left. Abby exclaimed, "Good boy!" and gave him a treat from the left. Then we let him relax for a minute. I took him to the center again and did the same thing. It took about four tries for him to follow the command without thinking about it, then we did the same thing four times to the right, with me standing on his other side and Abby raising her right arm and saying, "Ned! Go right!" After those four, we did one more to the left, which he did fairly quickly, and one more to the right, which he did after hesitating. We petted him and praised him, and then I held his bucket of feed—just a little oats—while Abby threw the evening hay into the wheelbarrow. Dad still hadn't arrived.

Chapter 8

Abby's mom was cooking supper—chili, it looked like—and her dad was sitting at the table, going over bills. He turned them over when we came in the door after kicking off our boots. The clock above the door to the living room said 5:45. Abby's mom said to Abby, "Why don't you set another place?" As always, she was easygoing and friendly, as if no matter who you were, once you showed up, she would feed you. I asked if my dad had called, and she shook her head, then said, "But I wouldn't worry about it."

"The other night he got a flat tire."

It was still light out, but the sun had dipped behind the mountains.

I went on, "Mom's going to be mad if we aren't

home for supper. She's making pot roast." As far as I knew, she wasn't making pot roast, but pot roast is Dad's favorite food. I added, "And vanilla ice cream." She hasn't made ice cream since before we got Joan Ariel.

Abby said, "You should call her."

And so I did, but I got a busy signal. Things, I thought, were getting sort of mysterious, and if I did not make an effort to zip my lip, pretty soon I would be telling a scary story about a cougar jumping onto the roof of Dad's car and crouching there until . . .

We pulled out our chairs and sat down, and in order to forget about the cougar, I said, "Maybe I'll spend the night." I said this in an easy sort of voice, as if this were absolutely a regular thing to do, as if I were at Grandma and Grandpa's. Abby and her mom looked at one another. Her mom said, "Oh, I'm sure everything—"

But I interrupted her and said to Abby's dad, "Maybe you should sing a song."

He said, "Maybe I should." And then he sang, "Amazing grace! How sweet the sound that saved a wretch like me!"

I've heard this song a lot. It is like the national anthem of the town where I live, but I felt like I'd never really heard it before because of the way the words vibrated in the air. Even the curtains were fluttering. Well, maybe. "When we've been there ten thousand years, bright shining as the sun . . ."

And just like that, I put my face in my hands and started to cry. I don't mean boo-hoo, I mean just tears and having to wipe my face with my napkin. Nobody said anything, and he kept singing, "'Tis grace has brought me safe thus far, and grace will lead me home." I put my elbows on the table and squinched my eyes shut. What I saw in my mind was Ned, first trotting across the pasture, easy as you please, the sun glinting above the trees in the distance, the leaves with all their colors of green, and then that changed and Ned was in the jumping chute, cantering through an in-and-out, stride, jump, stride stride stride, jump, canter away, come down to the trot. Grace itself.

The song ended. I took my hands away from my face. Abby's mom handed me a Kleenex and said not to worry. I sighed and ate a few more bites of my chili and part of a corn muffin, and then the phone rang.

Of course it was Mom. Dad was sorry to be late; he was on his way; she had, really and truly, made some vanilla ice cream with Grandma, and there was plenty.

Of course I knew that something strange was going on, but as I was listening to Mom (with Joan Ariel babbling in the background), I looked at Abby's face, then her mom's face, then her dad's face, then at the deepening twilight out the window, which was beautiful, then at Rusty's face appearing in that very window as she put her paws on the windowsill outside and woofed one time. Abby's mom said, "She is getting so bossy!" and we all laughed.

When Dad had come, and I was going outside, Abby was holding the door for me, and she said, "You should spend the night sometime," and her dad barked, "Yes! Then you'll find out how much work all these horses really are!"

I said, "Next week?"

Abby said, "We'll see," and Dad even opened the car door for me, not like he was in a hurry, but like he was being especially nice.

And yes, he apologized—he'd lost track of the time, and then he was so hungry, and he did want to call, but he didn't have the phone number, and when he called Mom at home, her phone was off the hook because Joan Ariel was having a late nap. When he finally got hold of Mom, she said she would call the ranch, and yes, it was all fine. As long as there was nothing to be scared about, I didn't care, because I could close my eyes and think of that song and imagine Ned gracefully cantering here and there, switching leads, jumping, easing down to the walk and *sauntering* away. "And grace will lead us home."

I said to Dad, "What's your favorite old song?"

"I have lots of favorites. Let's see. I guess when I was your age, it must have been 'Ain't Misbehavin'.'" And then he began to sing. He doesn't have a very good voice, so I interrupted him: "Can you play that on your trumpet?"

"I can."

But it was too late for trumpet playing when we got home—Joan Ariel was asleep, and our town was quiet. We ate ice cream and I went to bed. When I was walking up the stairs, and then brushing my teeth in the bathroom with the door open, I could hear Mom and Dad talking about something, and talking and talking, but I didn't listen. I was too tired to care.

The next day was really boring. Grandma and Grandpa had gone to meet some friends who were visiting from Florida. Their friends had decided to take two rooms for the weekend in Carmel, at some fancy hotel, and have Grandma and Grandpa stay with them and show them around the mission and all of those places. Grandma had spent a week deciding what to wear, and even went to the department store with Mom and looked at the racks of dresses. Every single piece of advice that Mom tried to give her she would not take, and even when Joan Ariel pointed and pointed at something, she still wouldn't buy it. She said there was nothing there for an old lady to wear, and finally pulled out her favorite black sheath dress, which she got before I went to kindergarten.

We had tuna fish salad for lunch—we had to save the ice cream for dinner—and I did not have a book to read. For a while after lunch, I did watch Jimmy Murphy pull Brian up the street in a wagon, then turn the wagon around and let it go a little ways down the street—maybe four or five feet—before catching it again and pulling it a little farther up the street. Every time Jimmy let the wagon go, Brian threw his hands in the air, grinned, and screeched like he was on a carnival ride. But Jimmy Murphy's motto was still "Ain't misbehavin'," I thought, because he played with Brian for a long time. When Jane came out, she gave him a list and some money, then took the handle of the wagon, and he walked up to the corner and turned right. He would be going to the market, and I wished I could go along, but I didn't have my shoes on, so I couldn't catch up with him, and I didn't know how to get myself invited anyway. I looked at the cartoons in the Sunday paper, but that never takes any time. I closed my eyes.

Ned said, "I'm lonely." He appeared under one of the trees, half in the shade.

I said, "I am, too."

He said, "I'm bored."

I said, "I am, too."

He said, "I want to go away."

I said, "Blue would trade with you."

"Where's Blue?"

"He's at the stables. It's big and busy and there isn't much turnout. Horses who live there have to be ridden four times a day."

He said, "I would like that."

I said, "I don't believe you."

He walked away. I opened my eyes. Mom said, "Oh, I didn't mean to wake you."

"I wasn't asleep."

"Well, you had your mouth open and you were snoring."

If it was all a dream, then it was a good dream.

Mom said, "You want to go to the library? Don't you have some book to return?"

"Man o' War."

"Let's go, then. If Joanie wakes up, your dad can give her her bottle."

I went upstairs to get the book. I didn't know what book I would borrow to replace Man o' War, but lots of times I just close my eyes and run my hand along the books and pull one out. This time, Mom was with me, so when my hand landed on something, I felt her push it a little ways to something else. What it ended up on was a book called The Incredible Journey, not a horse book, but with two dogs and a cat on the cover. I said, "What was the first one I touched?"

She pointed to White Fang. I had tried White Fang over the summer. Just about every animal in that book killed another animal. I couldn't get past fifty pages. She got a book, too—Little Women. She said that she wanted to read it again, because she hadn't read it since she was my age, but I knew that what she really wanted was for me to read it. I don't have to read it on my own, though, because in our fifth grade, you read it for school.

Mom likes to go to the library in a loop—on the way to the library, we walk down our street, across the street where the department store is, then over three blocks. On the way home, we walk up the street where the market is, but also a shoe store and a dress shop and a hardware store. It wasn't until we'd gone into the shoe store for a look, then bought some green beans, a loaf of bread, and oranges at the market and were walking home that she started telling me. The first thing she said was, "Sometimes I think a supermarket would be fun."

I wondered why.

Then she said, "Sometimes, really, I think it would be fun to live somewhere where everyone doesn't know every little thing about you."

I said, "How do you make friends, then?"

"You just do. You have neighbors and you meet people. You go to school. It can take a while, but it's a change. Maybe a change is good."

I said, "We change our classmates every year, but it doesn't seem like much of a change."

"Did you get anyone new this year? I mean from a completely different place."

"Like Florida?"

"Yes. You know, the Martinezes lived here for fifty years and they up and moved to Florida just out of the blue, and they've made lots of friends."

"Do they miss Grandma and Grandpa?"

"Well, sure, but now they have friends in more than one place."

I thought about her question. I couldn't think of any new kids, at least in our class.

"I wonder if Ruthie is moving to Florida."

"I doubt it. Maybe her aunt is taking them to Oregon. I heard she was living up there for a while."

We kept walking. Mom switched the bag from her right arm to her left. I held out my hand and she gave me her book. I was thinking about Ruthie in Oregon. I haven't ever read any book about Oregon, but I know that the capital is Salem, because we had our state capitals test in September (I missed two, South Dakota and North Dakota, because I got them mixed up—South is Pierre and North is Bismarck). When we turned the corner toward the school and our house, I said, "Dad moved. He has friends."

She said, "He did move." Then she said, "Your dad is a restless man. Maybe that's why he likes cars so much. Always looking for another view. He never takes the quick way on his sales trips—always the scenic route. That's how he got that flat the other night. He was trying out some ancient mountain road and it got dark and he hit a cattle crossing faster than he should have."

Now I remembered when my grandparents were here in the summer, and what I heard out my window. I said, "Would he go back there where Gran and Pop live?"

"Oh, goodness, no. He would never go back to somewhere he's been before, especially when the whole time he was there, he was dying to get out. He grew up downtown, you know, and he used to tell me, 'One danged street after another! What a nightmare! Here it's this street and then that street, and then the ocean, or then the forest, or then the rolling hills.'"

"Is he dying to get out of here?"

She looked at me. She didn't say anything, but she lifted her eyebrows. We came to the school, crossed the playground, went out the front gate, and headed down our street. The fog was coming in, and you couldn't see the ocean. Mrs. Murphy was on her front porch, about to ring the bell that calls her children in, so Mom put the groceries on our step and walked over to chat with her. I went inside. It seemed like we'd been gone a long time, the way it does on Sunday, but Joan Ariel was still yawning from her nap. Dad was sitting in the easy chair with her on his lap. The bottle, still full, was on the coffee table. Dad yawned, too, so wide that I saw the gold tooth that he has in the back twinkle. He said, "So, Ellen, what's for dinner?"

I named my wish: "Ice cream first, then blueberry pie, with a peanut butter sandwich for dessert."

He said, "Sounds good!"

Joan Ariel didn't cry, but she did turn her head and look at the bottle, and that made me think that she was really smart.

What we actually had for dinner was some ham and sweet potatoes and beets. There was ice cream for dessert, though.

I know what Mom and I were talking about. Dad wants to move and Mom isn't so sure, and yes, our town is very small and Grandma and Mom talk sometimes about how everyone has a finger in your pie and an eye out for whatever you're doing, and maybe the gossip trail is for getting into your business as well as for finding out what other people are doing—the gossip trail runs both ways. But here we are in our house. I've never lived anywhere else, and I've only ever been somewhere else maybe five times in my life—three times to where Dad grew up, once to Yosemite before I could really remember it, and once with Grandma and Grandpa to San Francisco, where the hill we drove down was so steep that Grandma just put her hands in front of her eyes and said in a low voice, "Dear God, please don't let the brakes fail."

When I woke up the next morning and was putting on my socks, I thought of Melanie, who goes to camp every summer, and I decided that I would ask her about it.

Chapter 9

On Monday, Ruthie had not disappeared, but she might as well have, for all that she said. And I didn't say anything to her—I didn't tell her to pull up her socks, or push her hair out of her face or button her blouse or wipe her nose. All of these things were done, which I considered to be evidence that my training method, as Abby would say, was working. What I did was tag along with Melanie all through recess and into the lunchroom, and what Ruthie did was tag along with me. Ann was spending all of her time with the three best friends who were always fighting. Now that there were four of them, it didn't matter so much that they were always fighting, because it was always two against two and never two against one. Who the twos were changed, though. Ann told me that they spent a lot of time talking on the phone, which her mom didn't mind but would have driven my mom crazy. I didn't get the sense that Ann didn't like me anymore, more that she was trying something else out. I didn't care. Ann is a regular person, not nearly as interesting as either Melanie or Ruthie.

Melanie opened her paper bag and took out her lunch, then flattened her bag on the table and set her lunch on it—liverwurst sandwich, reddish pear, two celery stalks, carton of milk. I did the same—chunky peanut butter and Grandma's raspberry jam, tangerine, oatmeal cookie, which I split with Ruthie, but she did have a salami sandwich. I know she was listening when I asked Melanie, "So tell me again where your summer camp is." I added, just to be polite, "I might go to summer camp next year."

"I went two years to a camp in the Sierras, and then last summer I went to a camp in Wisconsin."

Capital, Madison, but I had only the vaguest idea where Wisconsin was. I said, "How long does it take to get there?"

"Well, I took a plane to Chicago, then I spent the

night there, and my mom's cousin drove me to camp, maybe five or six hours."

"Why did you go there?"

"They have a canoeing program. You learn to paddle canoes, and then you go on overnight trips in the lakes, and they also have sailing."

Now was the time. I said, "Name five places you've been."

"Oh, let's see. Well, Lake Tahoe, Yellowstone, Chicago, Toronto, up in Canada, and New York City. Those are the first ones I can think of." She ate half of her sandwich, then said, "I was born in Washington, DC, but I can't remember it. Does that count?"

"It counts." I glanced at Ruthie. She was staring at her half of the cookie.

I said, "Why stick around here, then?"

"I don't know how long we will stick around here. If my dad gets a raise or a promotion, he usually has to move somewhere else."

I think her dad works for a newspaper. I said, "So, what's one good thing about each place?"

Now Melanie smiled. She didn't even have to think about it. She said, "Lake Tahoe, skiing; Yellowstone, the geysers; Chicago, going to the beach on Lake Michigan, near my cousins' apartment; Toronto, going to Niagara Falls, which is where we went before we crossed the border; New York City, not the Empire State Building, but walking down Fifth Avenue."

"Is it a hill?"

"No, absolutely wide and flat, with something to look at every single step."

"Where do you want to go?"

"New Orleans. London. Paris. My dad says Oaxaca, but every time he says it, my mom says Oahu."

I'd heard of New Orleans, London, and Paris, but not the other two. I said, "Have they been there?"

"Not yet. I hope we go, though."

I saw that Melanie, who sits right next to me every single day, had a life that was completely different from mine. That thought sort of made my skin tingle.

Now Ruthie wiped her lips (she'd finished her cookie) and said, "I want to go to the moon."

Melanie said, "They aren't going to do that, because of that fire." I didn't know what she was talking about, and I didn't ask.

Ruthie said, "Somebody will do it."

Melanie said, "My grandparents went on the SS *Normandie* for their honeymoon."

I said, "What's that?"

"An ocean liner. They crossed from New York City to France, stayed in Paris for a week, then crossed back in five days. My grandmother said it was the most luxurious thing she ever did, and even though they could barely afford it, she was always glad they did it."

The thing about Melanie is that she just says things. She never sounds like she's bragging. Since I always sound like I'm bragging, I don't understand how she does it.

We went out to the playground. A bunch of girls were skipping rope, so we got into that line. Two of the teachers were twirling the rope, and each of us had to run in, jump five times, and run out—then six, then seven. By the time the bell rang, I was panting, but at least we didn't have to do double Dutch, which I think is impossible, but Melanie probably likes it because she has been to Holland and, in fact, I decided, spent three weeks there wearing wooden shoes and doing ballet at the same time, and once I had imagined her doing lots of kicks and splits in wooden shoes, every time I saw the back of her head across the room, it made me smile.

On Tuesday after school, the phone rang, and when I picked it up, Abby said, "Hello. This is Abby Lovitt. May I please speak to Mrs. Leinsdorf?" Her voice was stiff and a little high, as if she were calling from my school, and I almost laughed, but instead, I said, "Certainly you may. I will get her." As I was putting the phone down, I heard her giggle.

Mom left me with Joan Ariel, who was lying on her back on her changing table, playing with a toy. It was a ball that could spin inside a hoop, and she would hold it in her right hand, spin the ball with the left, and then pass it to her left hand and wave at the ball with her right. I did my best not to do it for her, but it was hard. I opened my ears as wide as they would go, but I couldn't hear a thing. When Mom came back, she said, "Miss Ellen, you have been cordially invited to spend the night at the Lovitts' place on Friday night. When Mrs. Lovitt drives Abby to the stables Saturday morning, she'll take you for your lesson, and then somebody will pick you up after your lesson."

I said, "Whoever doesn't get a flat tire."

She said, "Exactly."

Joan Ariel tossed the toy over Mom's head. Mom said, "How did I get two real characters out of two?"

"Luck?"

"Yup." She kissed me on the forehead, then she kissed Joan Ariel on the cheek.

I said, "Were you always a good girl?"

"You'll have to ask Grandma. I'm not saying."

She put Joan Ariel against her shoulder, so I could make funny faces at her as they went down the stairs. Then I turned to go into my room and do my homework, but I went into Mom and Dad's room instead.

The good thing about Mom and Dad's room is that it is pretty big and has two sets of windows—one faces across the street and one faces the house next door, but since we live on a hill, it looks over that house and down the street. If the weather is really clear, you can just see a bit of the bay in the distance. The bad thing about their room is that they can't see the garden or smell it. They have a big double bed with a patchwork quilt on it, lots of colors. My mom calls the pattern "rippling waves," and we aren't allowed to sit on the bed. She and Grandma made it before I was born, when they were in a quilting group at the church. On Mom's side of the bed were two books, Dr. Spock and a thick book called *Topaz*. On Dad's table was only one book, *National Geographic Atlas of the World*. I'd seen it over and over and never once looked at it. What I did was sit down on the floor by the window, cross my legs, and open it up. It's heavy and big, much bigger than the social studies book, and the pages are shiny. The main thing is that a lot of the pages are mostly blue. The other thing is that when I finally found our town (not easy), it was very very small. It was so small that I pushed the atlas off my legs and stood up, then went to the window and looked down the street just to make sure that it was still there. And it was. Jane and Jimmy Murphy were walking down the street with Brian between them, and someone on a three-speed bicycle was coming up the street about as slow as a turtle, but he was leaning forward and panting. I sat back down and set the atlas on my knees again, but then Mom was in the room. She came around the bed and said, "What are you doing? Didn't you hear me call you?"

I shook my head.

"Why . . ." But then she saw the atlas on my lap. She said, "We can take that downstairs and put it on the coffee table. It's way too big for bedtime reading. Anyway, come set the table. I made spaghetti." She zipped out the door because she doesn't ever like to leave Joan Ariel alone, which is good for me, because I like to be alone as much as possible.

I left the atlas on the floor. After dinner, I took a book off my own shelf that I'd read three times, *King of the Wind,* and, this time telling Mom, I went upstairs and looked at the places that were in the book: Windsor, Ontario (near Toronto); Morocco; France; England. I turned the pages back and forth and tried to imagine those places, but what I really wanted to do, now that I had read about Sham again, was to see Ned. According to Abby, all Thoroughbreds, like Ned and Ben and Jack So Far, are descended from three Arab sires—the Darley Arabian, the Byerley Turk, and the Godolphin Arabian, who is Sham in the book.

Dad was home by the time I walked in the door from school on Friday, a little early, but good for me. I'd already packed my overnight bag three times, but I ran upstairs and packed it again while Dad sat at the kitchen table and ate the last of the ice cream. Soon we were on our way to Abby's, and it was a little different from the way it usually is. Dad was wearing his suit, and he was quiet while I told him why his atlas was on the coffee table, and gave him a little list of all the maps I'd looked at since Tuesday and what I thought about them. I had been writing them down in alphabetical order, but I didn't have to look at the list—once I write something down, I remember it. I think we'd just passed the airport (because I saw a plane gliding down out of the off-and-on clouds above us) when he said, "Jamaica. I would go there."

Jamaica is an island over near Florida. I said, "Would you go there first or Oahu first?"

"I would flip a coin."

I said, "Jamaica looks like a seal and Oahu looks like a hat."

"Well, our peninsula looks like a big face with its mouth wide open, screaming."

And it does. And we live on the top of its head, right under the brim of the clown hat.

Dad dropped me off and put my overnight bag on the porch, because we had to get right to work. He was smiling when he waved good-bye.

No one had to tell me that staying at Abby's was going to teach me a lesson. And it did teach me some lessons:

1. It taught me that the horses, all the horses, really like you when you're bringing them their hay. They nicker and even whinny, and they look at you like you are their best friend forever.

2. It taught me that walking around late in the day, when the sun is balancing on top of the ridge, and you can hear the birds calling in the trees, and you can see a hawk arcing through the sky with its wings wide, is much more pleasant than division problems.

3. It taught me that of course you have to watch out for the manure and not step in it, but it also has a pleasant, almost sweet odor.

4. It taught me that you can whistle while you work, like in *Snow White*, but you can also sing a song, and I did sing a song—"Lorena." When you carry the hay and sing a song at the same time, you feel like you are dancing.

5. It taught me that when you come in from doing your work, dinner tastes really good, especially if it's beef stew, which is what Abby's dad likes to have on Friday nights.

6. It taught me that it isn't bad to go to bed early. I stayed in Abby's room, in her other bed, and

before we went to sleep, we opened the window and looked at the horses in the pasture and the moon that was almost full and the brighter stars, and we made ourselves very quiet so that we could hear the horses walking in the dry grass, and blowing out air, and even their tails swishing, and a squeal or two.

7. It taught me that if you listen to those noises and make up your mind that everything is fine out there, nothing to worry about, you can sleep like a log all night and wake up first thing and be set for more work.

Chapter 10

Schooldays, Abby has to get up before dawn every morning, but we just rolled out of bed, put on our clothes and caps, and headed out the door without even brushing our teeth. The horses don't care. They care about the hay, and they were wide awake, much more wide awake than we were. We had already put their hay in the wheelbarrow the night before. After we pushed (Abby pushed, I helped a little) the wheelbarrow to them and threw out the hay, we refilled the water buckets with a hose and then were careful to turn off the spigot, because all you have to do in Abby's neighborhood is look at the hillsides, which are dry and gold, to know that water is very precious and you really can't wait for the rainy season to begin. Nobody had stayed in the barn overnight, so there was no cleaning in there. Abby's place is not like the stables, and other fancy barns, where the horses are in their stalls all day and all night, every day. That's why Blue prefers Abby's, and why wouldn't he? As I was walking around, I was saying to myself, "Ned, you are crazy if you want to leave here and go there," and yes, Ned did say, "I just want to go someplace new!" But when I looked over at him, he was busy eating his hay and it didn't look like he had said a thing.

We were back in the house by 8:15 (I looked at my watch). Abby's dad was sitting at the table and her mom was dishing scrambled eggs out of the frying pan (I hate scrambled eggs), but then I saw pancakes (which I love) and sausage and a plate of orange slices, and so, since I was hungry, I sat down ready to dive in, but Mr. Lovitt's hand shot across the table and landed on my hand just as I was poking my fork into the first pancake. He gave me a no-no look, and then closed his eyes and said grace. I was really hungry, so it seemed to last forever, and I must have snorted or something, though I didn't mean to, and after he said "Amen," he said, "Saying thanks is good practice," so I said, "Thanks!" And then he said, "Try saying it like you mean it."

I thought of Melanie, who is the best thank-you sayer I know. I imitated her. I said, "Oh, thank you," and then I smiled.

Good enough. We started eating.

But he wasn't in a good mood, humming a sad song. He was totally quiet and his eyebrows were lower than I had ever seen them, and Abby's mom was not in a good mood, either, I noticed, in spite of the pancakes. Abby looked from one to the other and back. I had no idea what was going on. We ate and ate, then cleared our plates, and I was really glad to go out to the barn and clean tack. Abby was sad, too, much quieter than she had been when we first got up, so I started talking and babbled on for a while about Melanie and Ruthie and how Ruthie was going to learn to do the splits and also to bend over frontward and put her head all the way between her knees (I saw a picture in a bookstore of someone doing that), but then I finally said, "Please tell me what's going on."

"My mom is going to an antiwar rally. Dad tried to talk her out of it, but she's made up her mind."

"How is Danny?" Her brother, Danny, is a soldier in Vietnam.

"Fine so far."

"Would Danny be sad that your mom is going to an antiwar rally?"

"Danny always says you should do whatever you want to do, because he always does whatever he wants to do. Or he did. I don't know if he does that in the army. I doubt it."

We kept soaping.

We never talk about the war at my house. Mom is against it, Dad says you have to do what you have to do, Grandma says that it could be worse, look at the Second World War, and Grandpa says it is bad, but also it's like a pressure valve that makes sure there isn't a much bigger explosion. When we came out of the barn with the halters and lead ropes to go get Sissy and Gee Whiz, I saw Abby's mom leave in their car. She waved out the window and drove off. Here is another lesson I learned about work—it takes your mind off stuff that is sad but that you can't do anything about.

Sissy and Gee Whiz were, of course, in separate pastures—Gee Whiz was in the gelding pasture on the left side by the hill as you walk out, and Sissy was in the mare pasture on the right side. The mare pasture slopes down toward a creek that runs in the winter, the spring, and for a while in the summer. The fence is on the other side of the creek, so the mares get to go stand in the water when they feel like it, and when Abby and her dad get a new horse, they teach it to cross creeks by walking around in and out of the creek and across it until it is no big deal. Sissy was standing by her gate, but lucky for me, Gee Whiz was way in the back, so I went in with Abby and dawdled behind her, and sure enough, Ned came trotting over, and guess what? I did have a lump of sugar in my pocket that I'd found in the tack room, and as soon as he got to me, I gave it to him and patted his nose. He seemed in a good mood, and while I was following Abby, he followed me—not too close but as if he was on a lead rope. I would stop and he would stop, and I would start up again and he would start up again. I didn't say anything to Abby, who was pretty far in front of me and finally whistled for Gee Whiz, and though he looked up, he didn't come. I guess that Gee Whiz is a lot like Danny.

Here's the thing about Abby—she's very patient. Here's the thing about Gee Whiz—he's got his own ideas. He spent most of his life being a successful racehorse—not great or famous, but he won a lot and traveled to a lot of racetracks, and so you could say that, for a horse, he saw the world. Sometimes he comes running straight at Abby like he's going to run her down, and then he stops dead about two feet in front of her and pricks his ears, and his face says, "Scared ya, didn't I?" Once last winter he even came to a sliding stop like they do in baseball games. Didn't touch her. Abby says that he knows where every part of his body is every moment and that's why he never ever knocks a rail when he's jumping. I suppose he figures that he's got better things to do than go around the arena with Sissy.

All this time, Ned was standing beside me, just standing. A couple of times he looked over at Gee Whiz, a couple of times he looked up the hill, a couple of times he put his head down and found some herbs in the grass. He snorted away a fly and tossed his head. But the whole time, he seemed relaxed, and after a minute or two, I started to pet him. Horses have all different kinds of coats, and Ned has a silky one, so you start petting him and then you don't want to stop. I tickled around his eyes and stroked the side of his face, but then I just started running my hands down his neck, over his shoulder, along his back and side. He dropped his head and half closed his eyes. His ears flopped. I kept doing it, then went around and started on the other side. In the meantime, Gee Whiz had walked even farther away, and I saw Abby go to the gate and let herself out. Now I closed my eyes a little, and after I stopped looking at Ned, I started feeling him—how warm he was, how big he was, the ripple of his muscles. I do not know how long this went on, but suddenly, Abby was saying, "Are you asleep?" I opened my eyes. There she was with Gee Whiz all haltered up and on the lead rope—and with that "Who, me?" look on his face like the boys in my class get when the teacher suddenly whips around and stares at them. Ned backed off.

But then he followed me as I followed Abby and Gee Whiz to the gate, and when we got there, he came closer, and I did give him another lump of sugar that I seemed to have found in my pocket. He stood there until I had Sissy, and then wandered away.

Can a horse be your friend? Books say yes, Abby's dad says no. Sissy, I'm sure, says, "I doubt it." As soon as I got on her, I could feel that I would need a crop to get her to make an effort. Why was that? It was a little warm but not hot. Was she stiff because she'd had a bad night? Was she tired or lazy or in season? Her ears were not pinned, but she kept putting them back a little. Was she warning me or just saying something that I couldn't quite understand? Abby saw me kick her a couple of times, took Gee Whiz over to one of the jump standards, got a crop, and brought it to me. I said, "What's wrong with her?"

Abby said, "Lazy."

"What if something hurts?"

"The more she moves, the less it'll hurt."

I took the crop, held it with the lash pointing upward rather than down, and Sissy woke up—she lengthened her walk, lifted her head. After a few steps, she went up into a trot, as if to say, "See? Please don't smack me." I didn't. The more we worked, the more agreeable she got. And Gee Whiz, who hadn't wanted to be caught, was perfect in every way—every transition was precise, every turn was elegant, every halt was square. Not a single toss of the head, not a single switch of the tail. And I could see that he was holding the bit in his mouth as if it were made of glass and he didn't dare break it.

The "lesson" part of my lesson was short. Once we were all warmed up, Abby set some courses. She jumped them first, then Sissy and I jumped them, and it did seem as though Sissy learned from watching Gee

Whiz. At least, her ears were pricked, she turned her head to see where he was going, and when we did our courses (Abby lowered the rails from 3'6" to 2'6"), they seemed easy. But then, I was watching, too, so maybe we both learned.

Afterward, when we were *moseying* up the trail (I like that word better than "sauntering" now), I asked if a horse could be your friend. Abby looked at me for a long time (and yes, Gee Whiz tossed his head), and she said, "I say yes, my dad says, 'Not a good idea,' because it's a lot harder to sell a friend."

"Is Gee Whiz your friend?"

She stroked him along the top of his mane, nodded, and said, "For now he is. But he's an ex-racehorse who's been around. So I think he considers me his co-worker."

I was going to tell her about Ned, but I didn't. Instead, I said, "I think Sissy was watching Gee Whiz jump, and that's why she did such a good job."

"You did a good job, too. You prepared for the turns. You aimed straight for the fences. You sat up when you needed to, and you went with the motion."

"I know, but . . ." I remembered my manners. I said, "Thank you, but did Sissy learn?"

We walked along. The trail got a little narrow, so I fell behind, and I thought Abby had forgotten my question until we were untacking, and she said, "I think she did learn. I mean, everyone knows they watch each other and do what the others are doing. If Gee Whiz finds a great place to roll—nice and muddy—some of the others go right to that place after he's finished and get nice and muddy, too. When one of them snorts and looks up at something, others will do the same. In the mare pasture, all of them pay attention to what Happy is doing, but not so much to what Sissy is doing, so that shows something. I'm not sure that a mare would pay attention to a gelding, but Gee Whiz is older and bigger and more self-confident than Sissy, so maybe. Anyway, I learn stuff from them, and what I learn is that not everything grown-ups tell you about horses is right." And then she grinned, and then I heard the gravel crunch in the driveway.

When Dad was driving me home, I told him about some of my lessons, but not all of them. I said that I'd worked very very hard, though. He said, "No surprise there."

Chapter 11

This is what happened after we got home. Dad cooked some hot dogs on the barbecue, which I like much better than boiled hot dogs, and then Mom and I took Joan Ariel for a long walk—down to the department store, along the beach, back up to Grandma and Grandpa's, where we ate some banana bread just out of the oven and talked about where we would have dinner Sunday night, and what we would have, and I asked if there could be a vote about that, but no one answered me. Then we kept walking because Joan Ariel fell asleep and Mom said that she had to burn off that banana bread, so we went up a steeper hill than we usually do, and it was a cool day. When we got home, I started reading the atlas again, on the coffee table, but then I lay back on the sofa and fell asleep, and no one woke me up until dinner, which was chicken soup with dumplings, and by nine o'clock, everyone was in bed and sound asleep except me. I was wide, wide awake, and I had absolutely nothing to do. I sat in my room for a while, looking out the window at the moon, which was now full, and then at some clouds that began to come in, and finally, I did something I'd never done before—I tiptoed downstairs and turned on the TV. It was just time for something called the late movie, and guess what? The movie was about a horse, and was called *National Velvet,* and it was exactly the movie I would have wanted to watch, because it was exactly about whether a horse could be your friend or not.

There are some strange things in the movie. One is that the girl's name is Velvet and she has a sister named Malvolia, and I have never known anyone with either of those names. The horse is named The Pie, which made me think of Sophia's horse, Pie in the Sky. The horse in the movie looks a little like Gee Whiz—big and long-legged, but bright chestnut with four white stockings, not gray. And Velvet is a little like Abby, I mean that she doesn't seem to care how fast she goes, and a little like me, because she can't stop talking and wishing she had a horse. There's a trainer who is about the same size as Velvet, and, as Grandma would say, he leads her astray, because after she wins the horse in a raffle, he gets her to believe that she can ride this horse in a huge race and of course win, because whoever is the star always wins in the movies, even though in a horse show lots of different people win, and sometimes you like them and sometimes you don't. The horse lives right by her house, but she never cleans his stall and she never cleans her tack.

I was about three-quarters into the movie when Dad came downstairs, and he wasn't mad. He got himself a glass of milk and sat down, and then he said the funniest thing—he said, "You know where they filmed that, don't you?"

I said no. "But the Grand National is in England, and all those people have English accents."

"They do, but it was made at the end of the war, so they didn't film it in England, they filmed it around here. Out at the stables. Look at the backgrounds." And so I did, almost more than I looked at Velvet and The Pie, and sure enough, I knew I'd been there. It was strange to see all of that in black and white, and also on the television.

I said, "Did she really ride in that race?"

"No. The movie started out as a book, and it was made up, and then when they made the movie, they had a stunt double do the riding. You can't put the star in danger. She's too valuable."

"She seems a little hysterical to me. I would rather be a stunt double."

"Hysterical?" Dad laughed. "It is true that I have never seen you be hysterical. I think 'dedicated' is your word." Then he said, "Of course you would want to be the stunt double."

We watched to the end of the movie. The only other thing he said was that he wished he could afford a color TV. He didn't ask me even one time why I wasn't in bed. And he didn't tell me to go to bed when it was over at twelve-thirty in the morning. I just yawned and went to bed, and in fact, I fell right asleep, and when I got up, it was ten o'clock, and there was a note on the kitchen table saying that everyone had gone to church, and my breakfast was in the oven and don't forget to use a hot pad, and I didn't. I ate bacon and a waffle and threw away the eggs, and everything was so quiet that I would have said I could hear the waves hitting the beach at the bottom of the hill, but no one was around, so I didn't say it, and I also didn't say the waves were so big that they curled up over the department store and swept cars into the bay. But it was an interesting idea. I thought some more about *National Velvet*. I didn't see how it answered my question about whether a horse could be your friend. Velvet says lots of things about The Pie and how she loves him and how great he is, but he never looks at her, or comes up to her, or whinnies to her. He seems more like Tater than like Ned—a good horse who knows what he is supposed to do and does it. I wished I could watch the movie over and over, the way you can read a book, but you can't. If it comes to your theater or on TV, there you are, but you have no way to ask or to order.

Grandma and Grandpa came a little early, and they brought a big piece of salmon, fresh out of the ocean, caught by a friend of Grandpa's who fishes a lot even though he isn't a professional fisherman. Mom put away the chicken she was making and put the salmon in the oven. I like salmon, so I decided to sit at the table with my mouth shut, and wait for it to bake— it smelled good, and anyway, there were chocolate cupcakes that I enjoyed looking at, too. Grandma was bouncing Joan Ariel on her knee and making faces. She does one thing where she closes her eyes and her mouth and says, very quietly, "One, two, three," and then she opens her mouth and her eyes as wide as she can and exclaims, "Oh, my goodness me!" and Joan Ariel starts laughing and laughing. I do, too. Mom says that I always laughed at that one when I was Joan Ariel's age.

For about ten minutes, I thought everything was fine, and then I started paying attention. I could tell that Mom and Grandma were talking about that thing no one will tell me about. Mom said, "I promise you we aren't going there."

"It's such a good opportunity." Grandma sounded really sad.

"I promise you."

I said, "What are you promising?"

Mom put her hands on her hips, and Grandma made Joan Ariel laugh again. I decided that the best plan was to say nothing.

Mom went back to making lemon butter for the salmon.

Then Grandma said, like she just couldn't help herself, "Don't do this for us."

Mom shook her head and checked the salmon. We were quiet for a long time, so I got kind of jumpy and said in a loud voice, "Ruthie disappeared." Actually, she hadn't, but she had been so quiet on Thursday and Friday that she might as well have. Mom said, "I saw their stuff being moved. The man who lives on the bottom floor and owns the house, he was helping them. There wasn't much of it. One load."

Grandma said, "That must be a furnished place."

Mom said, "Must be."

I said, "Do you know where she's going?"

"No one does. Her aunt hasn't said a word about it to anyone."

I said, "I hope they move to Montreal."

Mom said, "Do you mean 'Mon-tree-all'?"

"Yeah." I had pronounced it "Mont-reel," the way it is spelled.

Grandma said, "You are a reader. For years, I thought you were supposed to pronounce 'often' as 'off-ten.' Your grandpa was the first person to correct me."

Mom said, "This is ready."

I carried the baked potatoes into the dining room.

It wasn't till I was in my bed with my door open into the hall and my ears wide that I heard anything else. Mom said something I couldn't understand, and Dad said, "Well, I don't think you should have made that promise."

Mom said something, and then Dad said, a little louder, "I haven't decided."

Then Mom said, loud enough for me to hear, "*We* haven't decided."

"Sounds like you have! And anyway, we have to do something! This can't last!"

Then Mom said, "Shhh," and I knew she knew I was awake. I slid down under my blanket and put my pillow over my head.

The next day at school, Ruthie *was* gone. She was not at her desk, and when I lifted her desktop, I saw that the inside was empty. When I asked Mr. Nathan on the way to lunch where she'd gone, he shook his head and waved his hands. Melanie didn't know, either.

I went to the school library to see if they had *National Velvet,* but Miss Perkins said that it had been checked out in 1962 and never returned, and she couldn't read the handwriting of the person who'd checked it out, so there was no way to find it. I thought about walking to the public library on the way home from school, but even though I can go there, I have to ask permission first, and I knew if I asked, Mom would say, "Why do you want to go there? You already have three books." And "What book do you want, again?" And even though Mom is very understanding, I wanted to have this as a secret, so I kept my mouth shut and drew a few pictures of The Pie running and jumping fences, and of Velvet sitting on him. I realized that secrets you don't want to tell because you want them to be yours are different from secrets you can't tell because they belong to someone else. The second kind just seem to be popping in your head like popcorn, so you get nervous and have to be careful, but your own secrets sit there quietly, and you can look at them whenever you want to and then put them away again.

And speaking of Jimmy Murphy's secret, the other thing about it was that Brian seemed just like his regular self. One time I asked Mary how he was, and she said, "Just as naughty as he's always been," and Brian heard her and stuck his tongue out at her, then turned to me and crossed his eyes, then twirled his finger by his ear, meaning that Mary was crazy. We all laughed, including Mary, and Brian jumped up and down. I have to say that Jimmy Murphy has stayed a good boy, though. It has been three weeks now since he threw the book, and even though six spitballs have hit him on the head, he hasn't tossed any back, and he hasn't stuck his foot out to trip anyone, either.

After school, I went out the back way, across the playground, and down the street. When I got to Ruthie's house, the one with the outside stairs up to the second floor, I walked back and forth in front of it, looking at everything. All the windows and the door were wide open. I could have climbed the stairs and gone inside. Everyone who knows me would think that I'd do that in an instant because I am so nosy, but just thinking about it made me a little scared. There were some boxes by the curb. I opened the lid of one and saw a shirt that Ruthie had worn for a while and I guess grown out of. The sleeve was torn. There was some other stuff, but I didn't poke around. I closed the lid and walked down the block and turned the corner. I wondered two things—was she my friend, and would I miss her? I didn't know the answer to either of those things.

That night I dreamt about *National Velvet*. Velvet was sitting on The Pie, and the wind was blowing through the trees. She was at the stables, and the colonel was in the background. He was yelling, but I couldn't understand what he was saying. I kept pulling on her leg, like I was trying to pull her off The Pie. The Pie just stood like a statue. I woke up and sat there wide awake for a really long time, so long that after I finally fell asleep, Mom had to get me up (I usually wake up by myself), help me get dressed, and shoo me out of the house with an English muffin in one hand and some money for lunch in the other, since we didn't have time to pack my sandwich. I yawned all through arithmetic, social studies, and reading. I might have even dozed off, because the room got kind of hot and I felt like I was waking up. But Mr. Nathan didn't say anything, and after lunch (they served hash, which I like) I felt back to my old self.

As I was going out the front door of the school,

Jimmy Murphy caught up with me and said, "Did you fall asleep before lunch?"

I said, "Maybe. What do you think?"

"Well, I was looking at you. Your eyes were open, and you were sitting straight up, but you were so still for so long that I thought you were going to fall out of your chair."

"You should have hit me with a spitball."

"I thought about it."

"Did Mr. Nathan look at me?"

"A couple of times, but then he saw Todd stick his wad of gum on the underside of his chair, so he got on Todd, and when Todd pulled it off again, it made this long string, and everyone was staring at that. Did you hear him say that Todd was going to have to come to school on Saturday and clean the bottoms of all the chairs?"

"No."

"I guess you were asleep, then."

"I guess I was."

"You're lucky you can do that. I wish I could do that. All day."

I said, "Do you know what happened to Ruthie?"

But I said it in a low voice, and Jimmy was already walking away. He didn't answer.

Mom was on the porch with Joan Ariel in her arms, and she looked at me like she had something to tell me. I went up the steps.

Chapter 12

She didn't tell me right away. She put Joan Ariel in the playpen. Joan Ariel didn't cry. Mom took my jacket and hung it up, then went into the kitchen and came out with my cookie and my glass of milk. She set those on the coffee table and sat down, then she sighed a big sigh, which made me sigh a big sigh, too. I don't know why that is.

After I ate all my cookie and drank half of my milk, she picked Joan Ariel up again and started bouncing her gently on her knee. Finally, she said, "Well, Ellen, I have something to tell you."

I said, "I know."

She said, "I'm sure you do."

But I decided that I didn't want to hear it, so I said,

"You know, I had a bad dream last night, and I stayed up so long afterward that I fell asleep at school, but Jimmy Murphy said that my eyes were wide open and I sat up completely straight, and even when"—I thought of a name—"Paulie Miller poked me with his pencil, I didn't fall over. How do you think I did that?"

She leaned toward me with a smile and said, "Honey, I don't think you did that."

I said, "Oh."

Before I could think of anything else to say, she said, "When your dad started out in the vacuum cleaner business, we knew it was a little iffy. We didn't think he would last in it as long as he has, but he's done a good job." She looked around. She said, "I mean, your dad was not cut out to sit behind a desk in an office—"

I said, "Do you remember that paper-doll book I had?"

"I do. You didn't like it."

"I would like it now."

"Ellen."

There was a long pause that was supposed to tell me to *be quiet*. I was quiet. Joan Ariel had fallen asleep. She was quiet, too.

Mom said, "Anyway, Dad has to get out of the vacuum cleaner business, and find something else to do, and I think the thing he has found to do is back east, where his folks live."

I said, "I know."

"How do you know?"

"I keep my wits about me." This is an expression Grandma uses.

Mom stared at me, then laughed. Joan Ariel squirmed in her sleep but didn't wake up. Then Mom said, "Well, yes, you do."

"When do we leave?"

"Oh. Well, I don't know. Your dad hasn't accepted the position yet. I just think that you should be prepared."

I said nothing and looked at the atlas on the coffee table. I knew that the place we were moving to would be really small but seem really big. I said, "Where would it be?"

"Pittsburgh."

"Is that where Gran and Pop live?"

"No. But the man who owns the company is friends with Pop. They went to college together."

My eyes went to the atlas again. Mom saw this, and opened the cover and found the page. There was

Pittsburgh, there was Philadelphia, where I had been three times. I said, "Are there horses there?"

"I'm sure there are."

But not Ned. Not Sissy. Not Abby. Not Gee Whiz. Not even Tater. I got up from the sofa and went upstairs to my room.

For the rest of the week, no one said a word about Ruthie.

I did not look at the map of Pittsburgh.

I did all my homework.

I did not fall asleep in school.

I didn't say anything to Grandma or Grandpa about Pittsburgh.

When Dad got home Thursday night, I did not know whether he knew that I knew. I didn't say anything to him, either.

One problem with talking all the time, even times when you don't realize you are talking, is that people don't really know what you want. You have said so many things that maybe they are confused, or maybe they don't believe you. Maybe that's why Melanie gets to do whatever she wants—she hardly ever says what she wants, so her parents are just glad that she wants something. Melanie is an only child, like I was before Joan Ariel was adopted, but I've gone the other way—I make sure they know every single thing that I want when I want it, and also when I don't want it any longer.

On Saturday, I decided to try something. Dad was in a pretty good mood—he'd already started on his second cup of coffee, and Joan Ariel had slept through the night and eaten a tiny bit of mashed egg for breakfast, which made everyone happy. The first thing I said, as we were backing out of our driveway, was, "I think I want to go to the Grand National."

Dad said, "That would be fun."

"I think I want to ride in the Grand National."

"Maybe someday they will let women do that." He turned right at the bottom of the street. He sounded like he wasn't listening.

I said, "I should take ballet lessons."

"You should."

"I could learn to do the splits and the backflip."

"Probably."

"Or diving. I bet I could do a triple."

"Eventually."

"Jimmy Murphy wants to be a racecar driver."

"I'll bet."

"I want to do that, too."

"Okay."

"I wonder if you could make racecars jump things."

"If you had a ramp. But probably not a car. A motorcycle."

"That sounds like fun."

"It does."

Finally, I said, "They should send a horse to the moon." Even I knew that this was a totally stupid idea.

Dad said, "They should."

And then we got to the stables. We parked, I got out of the car, and Dad wandered away. I understood right then and there that if you can talk them into everything, then you can't talk them into anything.

Abby was on a horse that I didn't recognize when we arrived. She waved, and I watched her for a few minutes in the arena. She was just doing circles. So I went into the barn, went to Tater's stall, found the halter and lead rope, and started getting him ready for our lesson. He was eating his hay, but he did what he was supposed to do—he lifted his head, let me put on the halter, and followed me out of the stall without even trying to grab a last bite. I took him to the wash rack and cross-tied him. He stood quietly. I brushed him, picked his hooves, took a few tangles out of his mane (I leave the mane combing to Rodney, because you don't want to pull too many hairs). Finally, I petted him down the nose and looked him in the eye (only one because you can't look a horse in two eyes—they're too far apart). I said, "Hey, Tater, maybe you need a friend, too. I don't really know how to be your friend, but I'll try." I didn't have any sugar or carrots, so I tickled him a little around the eyes and petted his neck.

When I put the saddle on, I was careful to tighten the girth slowly, and when I put the bridle on, I waited for Tater to open his mouth and take the bit, which he did. I made a fist and put it between Tater's cheek strap and his throat, to make sure that the throatlatch wasn't too tight, and then I put two fingers between the buckle of his noseband and the back of his head to make sure that that wasn't too tight, either. I petted him again. When I took the reins and began to lead him out of the barn, I saw Rodney standing there with his hands in his pockets. He said, "Aye, mate, you'll be puttin' me out of a job one of these days." I went over and kissed him on the cheek. No one will ever put Rodney out of a job.

Abby and the new horse were standing outside the barn, and the new horse was staring toward the forest, his ears like antennae, the way that horses always do when they first arrive, but Tater *moseyed* past him without a look. He did put his ears forward as we approached the arena. I said, "Well, maybe you are looking forward to something." And as I said it, I decided that I was, too. And so, very softly, I sang a sad song to myself: "As I walked out in the streets of Laredo, as I walked out in Laredo one day, I spied a young cowboy all dressed in white linen. . . ." We walked along on a loose rein, and then, without me asking, Tater went up into a nice trot along the far side of the arena, still on a loose rein, head down, relaxed. I posted, one-two, one-two, and pretty soon I realized that "The Streets of Laredo" isn't a trotting sort of song. It is three-four time, a cantering sort of song, and a few moments after that, Tater moved up into the canter and I kept singing and he kept cantering. It was an easy canter, still on a loose rein, and I didn't even see Abby come into the arena. She was standing in the middle when we came down to the walk, with her cowboy hat pushed back on her head. I walked past her, and she said, "That was lovely."

"I should have warmed up more."

"Tater is old enough to decide what he wants to do."

"I think he likes a loose rein."

"I think he does. Let's see." And then we practiced, first at the walk, me holding the reins as lightly as possible, just as if they were silk threads, getting Tater to turn both directions, halt, walk again, turn some more, circle. I could ask him by thinking of what I wanted him to do, or by twitching a finger, or by closing my elbow a little bit, or by looking in the direction I wanted him to go. He was not perfect. He responded best to a little elbow movement, which made it easy for me not to close my hands around the reins and pull. Then we tried everything at the trot. If someone had been looking at us, they would have thought we were just wandering around the arena, but I knew that we were *experimenting,* and I thought that it was really fun. We trotted and trotted and I sort of lost track of the time. That song was in my head, and eventually it said to me, "Canter," and so Tater went up into the canter, and we experimented at the canter, too. Abby might have been saying something, but there was a breeze, and anyway, the song was in my mind, so I wouldn't have heard her, and the next thing that happened was that I sat up and bent my right elbow, and Tater cantered to the right, and just as I was thinking that we were on the left lead, he did a flying change and we were on the right lead, easy as pie, or, maybe, easy as Pie in the Sky. We then kept cantering as if this was no big deal, and at the end of the arena I bent my elbow, sat up straight, and went left, and after three strides, Tater did another flying change and we were cantering to the left. I went once around the arena—maybe Abby was clapping—and then I came down to the walk, walked over to her, and jumped off. I said, "I think we're finished."

"Don't you want to jump?"

I said, "No, I want to think about this forever and ever and ever."

"Well, walk him around a little bit. I don't have anything else for another half hour, so if you want to get on again, you can."

"Do you have a carrot?"

"I have a lump of sugar."

I held out my hand, then remembered to say please.

Tater was looking toward the barn like he didn't know what on earth a lump of sugar was, but he ate it happily enough once I gave it to him. I loosened his girth, then we walked here and there. Tater wasn't breathing hard. I petted him sometimes, and I thought about the house we would live in in Pittsburgh, much bigger than our house, and with a big lawn, and my room would be on the second floor, and Tater would live in the backyard, and of course I would ride him to school (which would be a block away), and then, because he's so smart, I would say, "Okay, Tater, go home and come back at three o'clock," and Tater would nod, and *mosey* away. His stall would be right outside the kitchen window, and we would keep the window open when we were eating our dinner, and Tater's bucket would sit on the table and he would eat with us.

And yes, I knew that this would never happen, but I knew that it should happen, that if it did happen, I would let all the kids in my school play with Tater, and pet him, and give him treats (but only healthy ones). When I got home from my lesson, I drew a picture of Tater putting his head in the kitchen window and turning it slightly to one side, as if to say, "I'm ready, where are my oats?" and after dinner (I said nothing about this) I went upstairs and fixed my picture a little bit here and there, and then I found a piece of tape and taped it to the back of my door so that when the door was closed, I could look at it. And then I closed the door, because I didn't want to hear another thing about where we were going and who was going to decide and why the vacuum cleaner business wasn't good. Was I now friends with Tater? I had to admit that I had no idea what he thought, but that I liked him better than I had liked him before.

Joan Ariel slept through the night again, that was two nights in a row, and when I was sitting at the table eating my cereal, she gobbled down her Pablum like she was starving to death, then ate some applesauce, and after that Mom handed her a zwieback and said, "Look when she opens her mouth. You can see a tiny little tooth popping out." And I did, and there was.

Chapter 13

Then, on Wednesday, at lunch, Melanie and I ate together, but we said absolutely nothing. Halloween was the night before. Grandma surprised me with a Heidi costume. Heidi is a girl in a book, who lives in Switzerland. Grandma loves that book, and I like it, but there are no horses. I trick-or-treated with the Murphys for an hour, but the hills in our town are so steep that I decided it wasn't worth it. We had already talked a little about Ruthie on Monday and Tuesday, but it seemed like there was nothing else to say, and so Melanie turned into the quiet one and I ate my peanut butter sandwich as if I were hiding in a closet. It didn't help that Ann and her friends were all getting along and having a wonderful time. After lunch, Melanie went to the playground, but I didn't follow her. I wandered here and there and tried to listen for some birds or maybe a horse (Ned) whinnying in the distance.

After school, I walked to the market with Jimmy Murphy and Brian and then carried home some of the groceries. I did all my homework, including an extra set of arithmetic problems, and then I fell asleep early, even before Joan Ariel, who I could hear babbling in her crib when I was lying on my bed. I woke up, or at least I think I woke up, and the reason I woke up was that Ned was saying to me in a very soft voice, "Where are you? Where are you? I wish I could talk to you."

He was under that same tree where he'd always talked to me before, and Gee Whiz was glinting in the moonlight a few yards away, maybe sleeping, because his head was down and his right hind leg was cocked. I thought that was why Ned was whispering, because of course Gee Whiz would be mad if Ned woke him up.

He said it again: "Where are you? Where are you?" And I didn't dare open my eyes, but I did whisper, "I'm here."

Ned tossed his head. He looked sleek and beautiful, very grown-up, and maybe he was, since he would soon be five (his birthday is in January).

He said, "There's a new horse here, and he wants to be the boss. He's not as big as Gee Whiz, and not as old, but he pins his ears and goes for him every time he sees him. Even Beebop wants to kick him." Even though Beebop was a bucking horse in the rodeo, he is as nice as can be; however, he is very successful at jumping forward and kicking so high he looks like he is going to flip over. If Beebop wants to kick you, you are in trouble.

I said, "You should stay out of his way."

"He always runs at you, even if you didn't do anything. He says there were seven horses where he was before, and he was the boss of all of them."

"I wonder where he was before."

"In a desert." I knew this couldn't be Arabia, but it did make me think of the Godolphin Arabian.

Now it happened—Ned ran away from where I was talking to him, and another horse, dark and shiny, chased after him, neck stretched out, teeth bared. He looked like that horse I'd seen at the stables. I hadn't seen much of him, but he had looked okay—pretty, calm.

I lay there with my eyes closed, waiting for Ned to

come back, or for Gee Whiz to offer an opinion, and the next thing I knew, it was light, and I was opening my eyes. I was on my side, and the door of my room was against the wall. Mom was in her robe, passing on her way to the bathroom. I pushed back the covers and sat up, looked out my window. Had I really been talking to Ned? Had Ned really been talking to me? Or was it a dream like my *National Velvet* dream—so vivid that it seemed to be happening, more vivid, in some ways, than most things that do happen?

All spring, I was completely sure that Ned was talking to me. I was nine then. I was in fourth grade. It's pretty clear when you're running around on the playground with the kids in fourth grade that they don't know what they are doing. After Ned stopped talking to me, I partly forgot about it and partly thought that I had made it up and partly decided that Ned was my dream and my way of talking to myself. Now here I was again and I didn't know.

I went to school. I did all my work. I turned these thoughts over and over in my head and didn't say anything about them. At lunch, Melanie and I talked about what she was going to do over the weekend—

go with her parents to San Francisco, to a play at the Geary Theater, which is very old, and then stay in a fancy hotel. She told me the name of the play, but I didn't pay attention. We said nothing about Ruthie.

Later, when I was setting the table for dinner, the phone rang. I picked it up, and it was Abby. She said, "Would you like to have an extra lesson at the stables? I'll be out there tomorrow afternoon. If you could get there right after school, we could work with Blue and Tater the way you did with Tater on Saturday. I really want to try it. I would start on Blue and you would start on Tater, and then we would switch, I hope more than once. I want to see how they deal with it, and I think it would be good for us."

I said, "I'll ask Mom. Dad won't be home, so she would have to drive me." Mom was now standing in the kitchen doorway. I said, "Can I have an extra lesson with Abby tomorrow afternoon at the stables? You would have to drive me, though."

Mom was already shaking her head before I even finished talking.

I said, "Or I could call Grandpa. Maybe he could drive me. It's only to the stables. . . ."

Mom was still shaking her head. And then she said the scariest thing. She said, "We can't afford an extra lesson. Frankly, I don't see how we can afford the lessons you're taking now."

There was dead silence. Or rather, I was dead silent, and Mom was dead silent, and Joan Ariel wasn't crying. I thought maybe it was my turn to do that.

After a moment, I realized that Abby was saying, "Ellen? Ellen?"

I put the phone to my ear. She said, "If you can get there, you don't have to pay. I think it's training, not a lesson. This is for me, not you. It can be free." I handed the phone to Mom, took Joan Ariel, and walked out of the room. She was getting heavier, but not as heavy as a saddle. I sat her against the arm of the couch and played patty-cake with her. I am sorry, I think I'm pretty smart, but between you and me, I think Joan Ariel is smarter. Mom walked through the living room and said only one thing, which was, "Okay." But she still looked sad. I kept playing with Joan Ariel, and Mom seemed better when she came down the stairs again. Grandma and Grandpa showed up for dinner and brought spaghetti and meatballs. The only happy person at the table was six months old.

I didn't dream about Ned again, or talk to him. When I got to the stables after school (Mom seemed more herself when she picked me up in Grandpa's car, and without Joan Ariel, so I guess she left her with Grandma), I asked Abby if the horse from last weekend had gone to live with them at the ranch.

"He's been there almost two weeks now."

"How's he doing?"

"I like him. He's very willing."

"Do you like him better than Gee Whiz?"

"I don't think so, but they're all different."

"Is he turned out?"

"Now he is. He was in for a few days."

"Is he getting along with the others?"

"Oh, yeah. He's very easygoing."

"Nobody's been hurt?"

"Nope." Then, "Well, Gee Whiz seemed a little stiff the other day, but he was over it the next morning."

"No marks?"

"Why are you asking?"

I pretended not to hear her and went to get Tater.

Rodney was nowhere to be found, so I wondered

if I had put him out of a job. When I went into the big tack room, though, his things—jacket, cap, boots that he calls "wellies"—were in the corner. I carried Tater's saddle, pad, and bridle to the wash rack and hung them up. Then I got Tater. I can't say that he nickered to me, or pricked his ears, or whinnied to me, the way Blue whinnied to Abby, but he did look at me, and then he moved one step toward the stall door as I pushed it open, and I guess that was hello. At any rate, it felt like hello, and of course he was a good boy and put his nose right in the halter. When I cross-tied him on the wash rack, I could see Mom outside, taking a little walk. She paused, put her head back, and took a deep breath, and yes, the piney smell at the stables is very nice.

Once I had him tacked up, I walked him to the front door of the stables, and there was Rodney, sitting on the mounting block, eating something. I said, "What's that?"

"A scone. A cuppa."

"What's a cuppa?"

"Why, miss, don't you know the proper word for tea?" He was making himself sound so English that I almost could not understand what he was saying.

He looked like he was about to laugh. Then he drank the last of his cuppa, wiped his mouth on his sleeve, came over, and tossed me onto Tater. He said, "I make me own scones, miss, and I will keep one for you till after your ride, because they are the best scones in America."

I will never understand how Rodney, who is just about the same size as I am, can throw me around like a basketball. But I said, "Thank you very much, Mr. Lemon. Your kindness is much appreciated." Then he did laugh, and so did I, and Tater jogged off to the arena like he couldn't wait.

Abby was already there, walking Blue on a loose rein, and Blue looked like he always does from a distance, very beautiful, pale gray with dapples, blue around the face and across the haunches, dark mane, dark tail. I saw that Abby was trying out our exercises, so I bent my elbows a bit and softened my fingers. Tater looked here and there, stopped, dropped a load of manure. Abby says that when a horse drops a load of manure, that means he is comfortable and relaxed. Tater ambled along. I sat deep, wiggled my shoulders a little, and took some good breaths. Tater sighed. I said, "Tater, don't do anything bad, because Mom is watching."

Tater's ears flicked.

But Tater never does anything bad.

And then he did.

I was walking along, thinking about my elbows, warming up. Mom was at the far end of the arena, and we were heading in her direction. Tater seemed relaxed, and maybe he was too relaxed, because just as Mom turned around to watch me (I could see the smile on her face), a bunch of crows flew out of a tree next to the arena, and straight at me and Tater. Tater spooked and spun right out from under me, and there I was, sitting on the sand of the arena. Tater ran off, Abby turned Blue around, Mom shouted, "Oh no!" and the crows, three of them, flew over the roof of the barn. Tater is very short, or, as Abby's dad would say, close to the ground. I stood up and brushed down my breeches. Just when I was thinking that nothing hurt, here came Tater, right over to me at a good trot. He stopped, stretched out his nose, and sniffed where I had my hand, feeling my lower back. It was like he was saying, "Are you all right? I am so sorry." He moved one step closer and put his head down. I took the reins with one hand—at least they hadn't flipped over his head, at least he hadn't stepped on them—and I patted him with the other. I said, "I am fine. I bounce."

I led Tater over to the mounting block, got on again, and started walking, just like nothing had happened. Mom still had her hand over her mouth, but I guess she had learned her lesson; she didn't say a thing. After that, we rode longer than we usually do, the same as before, easy to the left, easy to the right, easy up to the trot, easy down to the walk, easy up to the canter, easy down to the halt, look left, look right—fifteen minutes on Tater, then fifteen minutes on Blue, another fifteen minutes on Tater, another fifteen minutes on Blue. I would never have thought that you would have to get used to riding Blue, because he is so smooth. In fact, I thought I was used to riding Blue, but yes, he is a horse and Tater is a pony, and once I was used to Tater, Blue took some adjusting, and vice versa. What I learned was that Tater isn't uncomfortable, the way I thought he was a few weeks ago, he is just himself.

Himself, the pony who came over to see how I was after he dumped me. When it was time to get off, I gave him a kiss on the cheek, and I meant it. Abby got off, too, and ran up her stirrups. She said, just like she knew the answer, "You okay?"

"Yes."

"I thought so. You rode like you were okay."

"Thanks for not asking. I hate it when people ask you stuff all the time." I think Mom overheard this, because she was standing in the doorway of the barn, with her hand on her watch. She turned away. When I walked out the door, Rodney met me with a paper napkin wrapped around something. He bowed and presented it to me. Inside were two things, not one, that looked like biscuits. I found Mom in the car. She just said, "You did well, sweetie. I can see why you like to ride," and that was all. We ate the scones on the way home. They tasted much better than biscuits—sweet, not buttery.

When we got to Grandma and Grandpa's, they had already had supper, and Joan Ariel had eaten a zwieback, some strained peas, some mashed peach, and a bit of meat loaf.

"Meat loaf!" said Mom. "She's only ever had a little chicken."

"She loved it," said Grandma.

"She did," said Grandpa. "She said 'yummy.' I think that was her first word."

Mom didn't say anything after that, except to thank them for watching her. Grandma sent some meat loaf and potatoes home with us, and they were good. But I didn't say "yummy" out loud. I knew better, for once.

I did my homework and went to bed at nine-thirty, right when I was supposed to. To make myself fall asleep, I read the most boring book I could find on my shelves, *Five Little Peppers and How They Grew*. The story isn't bad, but it puts you to sleep because it goes on and on and on. I read it. I even read some of the pages over and over just to make sure that they would put me to sleep. And they did. And I did have a dream, but it was about driving on a road and stopping and asking people where Pittsburgh was, and nobody knew.

I woke up at one point, opened my eyes, and closed them again. I even whispered "Ned!" a couple of times, but Ned never showed up. I had some nice thoughts about Tater, though.

Chapter 14

At lunch on Thursday, I'd just sat down with Melanie and was pulling my peanut butter sandwich out of my bag when Jimmy Murphy walked over and stood there. I looked around. His usual friends were not staring at us, waiting to laugh, they were talking about something, maybe the World Series, because I think I heard the word "Gibson." Jimmy said, "Hey." When Melanie turned her head and stared at him, he pulled out a chair and eased himself into it. His sandwich was liverwurst. He said, "You going in the spelling bee?"

Melanie said, "I did last year."

"What was your hardest word?"

"'Derivative.'"

"What word won?"

"'Loathe.'"

"What does that mean?"

I said, "Hate. There's a more interesting word like that one. It's 'loath.' I am loath to sit next to your liverwurst."

They both gave me a laugh, then Jimmy said, "I want to go in the spelling bee."

I said, "I didn't know you could read."

"I'm a good speller. I've gotten an A on every test."

I have *not* gotten an A on every test. I focused on eating my sandwich, then peeling my orange, but of course I kept my ears open. Jimmy said to Melanie, "I think you could coach me." Then he smiled.

Melanie said nothing for a long time, not like she was insulted or anything, but just like she was Melanie. After a while, she said, "I could do that. I don't know when or where, though. I have dance in the afternoons three times a week, and I take diving lessons on Saturday."

Jimmy looked a little amazed by this. No Murphy ever does anything after school except run around the neighborhood and hope to stay out of trouble. I said to Melanie, "We live just down the street from you.

Jimmy lives across from me. You could walk home with us and we could think of words for Jimmy together. My favorite at the moment is 'mosey.'"

Jimmy said, "M-o-s-e-y. That's an easy one."

"Yes, but it sounds just exactly like what you are doing when you are moseying."

Melanie said, "Weird."

Jimmy said, "W-e-i-r-d."

And that was that. We decided to start that very day.

Which was why, at five-thirty, when the sun was going down, and Jimmy said that he would walk Melanie home from my house (she lives about four blocks away), I finally wondered for the first time why Dad wasn't around. Sometimes he was late, but when he was, he always called, and I hadn't heard the phone ring.

I went into the kitchen. Mom was giving Joan Ariel a bottle, and something in the oven smelled good. I said, "Where's Dad?"

"I'm sure he's just a little behind. He hasn't called."

And he didn't call. And he didn't come home. And we ate the short ribs and the baked potatoes by ourselves at the table, and about an hour after dinner,

Mom put what was left in the refrigerator with a piece of wax paper over it, and before I even asked her anything, she said, "I'm sure he's just had another flat tire somewhere. But the phone is on the hook. I checked. Don't worry!" But she said it in the way moms say that when they are worried.

And Joan Ariel, always a good baby, would not go to sleep. Mom put her down and picked her up and walked her around and put her down and picked her up and walked her around. She rocked her downstairs in the rocking chair, took her outside for some fresh air. Finally, she went into her own room and shut the door and just let her cry in her crib. I was supposed to do my homework, and there was a lot of it because Jimmy and Melanie and I had spent so long looking in the dictionary and coming up with words ("aggravation," "lunacy," "portion," "receive," "senate," "stentorian") that I hadn't done any right after school. I looked at the division problems. I looked at the reading assignment. I opened the social studies book. I spelled the words aloud in the list for the spelling test. But that was all. Finally, I got up and went to the window. I opened it and smelled what there was to smell, but most of the flowers were gone now. I tried to listen for the waves down the hill, and I tried to see an owl somewhere. There were a few sounds of trucks and cars going by, and someone on the street who I couldn't see shouted, "Hey! Frank! Wait up!"

Three times, I heard a car coming up the hill, but I never heard it slow down or turn into our driveway. I never saw brightness from the headlights flow into the backyard and then go away. Dad didn't drive in. I looked out the window as long as I could, then I got too sleepy to even get to my bed, so I curled up on the floor and fell asleep, but of course the floor is very hard, so I woke up in the dead of night. Everything was quiet, including Joan Ariel. I got up off the floor and tiptoed to my door, opened it very carefully, and tiptoed out onto the landing. Joan Ariel's door was open. She was lying on her stomach, sleeping. Mom's door was open. I peeped in. Mom was sleeping, too. On her back. Dad wasn't there. I stood on the landing for what seemed like a long time, looking down the staircase. I made up a story about how Dad was down there, asleep in the recliner, because he was so tired from a long day, and he had watched the late movie, and after that there was something called the late late movie, and he watched that, too. I coughed twice to see if I might wake him up, and then I listened for snoring, even though Dad doesn't snore very often, but everything was very very quiet, not even a single car coming up the street. I went into my room, took off my clothes, hung them up carefully to pass the time, and finally, I went to bed.

And he wasn't at breakfast. Mom gave me a written homework excuse—she said I was "under the weather" but that I didn't have a fever. Mr. Nathan, who is way nicer than Miss Cranfield was, told me I could make it up over the weekend, and when we went out for recess, I sat around talking instead of jumping rope because I thought that I should do my best to look under the weather (which was, by the way, damp and chilly and made you not want to do anything). But I did not say anything about my dad. That is a third type of secret—one that is yours, but one that you do not want to tell, even though other people might want to know. I thought that if Ruthie were still at our school, I might have told her, but she was gone.

It was Friday. I should have been looking forward to my lesson the next day, but the only thing I could think about was how I would get there, since Dad was always the one to drive me, and that led me to think about how if I couldn't get there, and we couldn't afford the lessons, then maybe that was the end of my lessons, and that led me to think about how I might never see Ned or Tater, or Tater or Ned (who was first? I didn't know anymore), or for that matter Abby, ever again, and then I thought something had happened to Dad, which seemed impossible at first and then not so impossible, and then I stopped thinking about it, but in order to stop thinking about it, I had to not look forward to my lesson, and so I didn't. I looked forward to doing a lot of homework over the weekend.

When the school bell rang, everyone jumped up and ran out—I usually did, too, but now I acted like I was feeling under the weather, and I was the last out the door, so that Mr. Nathan patted me on the shoulder and said, "Hope you feel better, Ellen." When I got to the front door, I saw Melanie's mom pull up in their blue station wagon, then I saw Todd do a chin-up on the fence that runs around the playground, jump down, and walk down the street that leads to the market. I thought about going to the market. If I'd had a quarter in my pocket, I would have gone with him, and bought some licorice and some Dots, anything to not go home. I saw Jimmy Murphy catch up with him, and after a minute, they started poking each other and laughing, and Jimmy swiped Todd's Giants cap. I sort of liked that, because it meant there was still a little of the old Jimmy left—just enough to make you believe the new Jimmy wasn't a robot the Murphys had decided to trade the original Jimmy in for. Some sixth-grade girls did a few cartwheels, and then I had to start walking, because it was almost three-thirty, and pretty soon the teachers would be coming along, asking me what was wrong and what I was doing. I went out the gate, crossed the street, and after all, I walked past our house. No car in the driveway. Mom wasn't on the porch or looking out the window, so I kept walking, down to the bottom of our street, and then I stood on the corner for a long time. Down the street, there was one tree in the way, but if I looked hard enough, I could just see the edge of the bay against the sky. I was not looking forward to one single thing in the whole world, not a riding lesson, not reading a book, not dinner, not seeing Joan Ariel, not buying anything at the department store. Even the house on the corner that I was standing beside, the prettiest house on our block, looked ugly. And then here came Mom, up the hill from the next block over, pushing the baby carriage, and she said, "What are you doing?"

I said, "What are *you* doing?"

She pretended that I wasn't being sassy. She said, "I was at the market, picking up a chicken. I left you a note."

"Can we afford a chicken?"

Mom stared at me and then said, "I shouldn't have said what I said the other day. I was just a little stressed. Yes, we can afford a chicken." We started up our street, which is steep. Joan Ariel was under her blanket, sleeping. After a couple of steps, Mom said, "This is what I learned from the Depression. I mean, I was five in 1932, so maybe I was too young to understand much, but I did understand that even when times were bad, there was always a way to make do. Somebody would think of something, even if it was just how to put some corn in the beans to make them taste better. Even if it was just telling a joke. Your grandma says I'm always expecting the worst. I am sorry for that."

Now we were standing in our driveway, our empty

driveway. I waved my arm. I said, "But he didn't come home."

Mom looked around, then said, "Oh my, yes he did. He got home about ten this morning. I forgot that you didn't know."

"Where was he?"

"I think I have to let him tell you. But don't worry."

"Can I go to my riding lesson tomorrow?"

"Of course. Now I'd better get this chicken into the oven." She lifted Joan Ariel out of the carriage very gently. I held out my arms and took her. She didn't wake up. Mom pushed the carriage up the steps, then came back for Joan Ariel. We carried the groceries and my books into the house. Mom laid Joan Ariel in the playpen, and still she didn't wake up. In fact, she snored two tiny little snores. It was amazing how normal everything seemed.

Friday! At last, moment by moment, I began to think about my lesson. First I would tack up Tater, then I would go to the mounting block, and Abby would be at the mounting block, getting on Blue, and then we would walk here and there around the grounds of the stables, bending our elbows, sitting deep, looking up, loose rein, light rein. Then we would go into the arena, and the jumps would be exactly right, and we would do two courses, Abby going first to the right, me going first to the left. Then we would take a long walk through the forest to the cove, and I would pretend that Velvet and The Pie were with us, and when we got to the cove, we would walk, then trot, back and forth where the sand was wet and hard, then we would amble, mosey, *meander,* back up the trail. I could picture it all perfectly right between Tater's ears. I went into the kitchen and found an apple, which I took upstairs and put with my jodhpurs, just to make sure that I would not forget it.

At six o'clock, when we usually eat, I went downstairs (and yes, I had begun on my makeup homework). The table was not set, though Joan Ariel was sitting in her high chair staring at the piece of zwieback on the tray and touching it first with one finger and then with the other. Whenever it moved, she giggled. I said, "How long does a chicken take?"

"It's resting. Anyway, we're going to be eating later from now on. Six-thirty instead of six, so be sure you have an extra cookie when you get home from school. You want a little something?"

"Why are we eating later?"

"Well, your dad has to drive at least half an hour every day back and forth to his new job, and that's if there's no traffic. So we have to practice being flexible."

"Where is his new job?"

"Didn't I say? I'm sorry. I hardly slept a wink last night." She kissed me on the forehead. And then she said the name of the town we pass through on our way to Abby's ranch.

Chapter 15

Dad's new job, which he told us all about when he got home, is at a car dealer. They also sell trucks—in fact, it sounds like they sell anything that moves, except horses. It is a big dealership, the same brand as our car.

I said, "What brand is our car?"

"Ford."

"I thought it was a Falcon."

"It is, but that's a type of Ford."

That made me feel like a dope, so I didn't ask any more questions. Dad ate both chicken legs and both wings and half the potatoes and even most of the spinach. There were no leftovers. I have maybe never seen him so happy in my life. He talked about all the people who come in looking because the dealer is right near the highway, and how great the repair shop is, completely up to date, and how he would be the one to take customers for test-drives, and how his new boss thought he was really good at explaining what was special about the cars. He said, "Believe me, cars are way more interesting than vacuum cleaners!" And they have nice names—Fairlane, Galaxie, Thunderbird, Country Squire, and, of course, Mustang.

When we got to the dessert, which was Grandma's lemon meringue pie, I said, "Are you going to miss driving all over the place?"

And Dad said, "Nope. What's going to happen is that I'm going to stop missing you and your mom and Joan Ariel. My customers can drive all over the place." He grinned.

I pushed the meringue part aside and ate the lemon part. It was delicious. But there were still things going on, because when I said, "So, we get to stay here," Mom and Dad looked at each other, but before they could say anything, just like she had been ordered to do it, Joan Ariel made a face, and then there was a stink, and Mom jumped up to go change her diaper, and Dad got up to clear the table. Here is a thing that

I do not understand—why don't they tell you things? They act like if you are ten years old and in fifth grade, you can't understand what is going on, but you do understand if you have a brain in your head. If our parents and grandparents and teachers and principals would eavesdrop on us the way we eavesdrop on them, they might be more willing to *communicate*. That was another word Melanie and Jimmy and I found in the dictionary.

After dinner, when Dad was sitting in front of the TV, sort of half reading the paper and half looking at a show, and Mom was putting Joan Ariel to bed, I said, "Where were you last night?"

"I was coming home from down south, and I stopped to talk about my new job at the dealership, but the boss had so many customers that he couldn't talk to me until late."

"Why didn't you call?"

He looked me right in the eye.

I said, "The phone was on the hook."

"I know." He closed his newspaper and shook his head a little, then he said, "I should have called. I knew that. But I wanted to give you and your mom good news, and I waited too long, and then I was afraid to call, because I didn't want to wake everyone up, especially Joan Ariel. I wasn't thinking, and I'm sorry." He took my hand and leaned forward. He said, "I really am sorry. I don't always do what I tell you to do. So if you remember this, what you have to remember is that moms and dads make mistakes, too, and then they have to answer for them, just like kids. Can you remember that?"

I nodded. I thought about the landing in the dark, peeping into Joan Ariel's room, peeping into Mom's room, looking out the window in the middle of the night, and how scared I was, but I decided not to tell him. Another type of secret—the one that is all yours and nobody else needs to know. Later that night, when I was lying in bed, I thought that I would really like to go back to being a kid like I used to be, when I didn't know or care about anything except when my riding lesson was, what was for dinner, what was on my Christmas list, and whether Ann and Todd were acting stupid or not. Now it seems as though I care about so many things that they all couldn't possibly work out.

The next morning, when Dad and I were driving to my lesson, Dad said that for a few weeks, just to learn the ropes ("What ropes?" I thought), he was going to work Monday through Friday, like a regular job, but then he was going to start having to work on Saturday, which would mean my lesson would have to change, but he was sure we could work something out—maybe a Sunday lesson.

I said, "Abby and her mom and dad go to church on Sunday."

"So does everyone, but . . ."

"All day. I thought you knew that."

"I guess I forgot. Well, something will turn up."

I decided to believe him.

We didn't have that lesson I'd imagined, but we did have fun. When I got there, Sophia was on Onyx, and Abby was on Gee Whiz. Abby's dad was leaning on the fence, watching them jump, tapping his foot, and humming. I stood beside him, and listened to his song, and when he turned to look at me, he did smile. I said, "After my lesson, will you teach me that song?"

He said, "Sure."

"What's it called?"

"'Foggy, Foggy Dew.'"

"Did they write it about this place?"

He laughed. He said, "No, but they could have."

"Abby said that you sing sad songs when you are happy."

He pushed back his hat, then he said, "Maybe I do, but the sad songs have the most beautiful tunes."

"Why?"

"I don't know."

Then we stood quietly and watched Onyx and Gee Whiz do their last courses. Gee Whiz knocked one rail over with his right hind foot; Onyx was clean. But I saw that Gee Whiz learned his lesson, because when he came back and did the jump again, he kicked out both hind feet, like he was saying, "I will never touch it again."

I said, "He's smart."

Abby's dad said, "Seems like it."

I went into the barn to find Tater. Rodney helped me this time, and when we were all tacked up, I went into the arena with Abby and Sophia. Now that I was sitting on Tater, I realized the jumps were really high—as high as Tater is, which is fourteen hands, which is 4'8". I was pretty amazed that Gee Whiz was jumping so high, even though Onyx does all the time. Abby seemed excited and calm at the same time—she was smiling a huge smile but riding along quietly, petting Gee Whiz a little on his neck. When she and Gee Whiz walked past me, he was on a loose rein with his head down, taking long, relaxed strides like he had never seen a racetrack in his life. I said, "Don't make me jump these jumps, please."

Abby said, "When you're ready, you'll like it." And I believed her, because she always tells the truth.

Now Sophia came back into the ring, this time on Pie in the Sky, who is a very flashy chestnut with four white stockings and a blaze. He looks as big as Gee Whiz, though I don't think he is, and as Abby left the arena on Gee Whiz, the horses passed each other and both of them flicked their ears backward, as if to say, "Watch out for me, buster!" I said to Tater, "What they don't know is that you are the best one," and I meant it. We ambled, sauntered, and moseyed around all of the jumps, and then we went up into a nice trot. Tater gave a few sighs, which meant he was comfortable, and as I trotted past Sophia, she said, "Is that pony always always good?"

I said, "Yes."

"Don't let him spoil you."

I said, "I'll try not to."

She was smiling, so I suppose she was joking, but Sophia isn't very good at making jokes. Tater and I kept walking and I was talking to us about something, maybe Dad's new job and how there should be a two-person car called the Ford Tatermobile. I could just imagine it—a sweet little bubble buzzing down the road, mine would be yellow. . . .

Sophia circled around me and said, "Can I give you some advice?"

Why not? Sophia wins more blue ribbons than anyone. I said, "Please do." I thought it would be heels down, thumbs up, sit deep, stay with the motion, watch where you want to go. Even as I was wondering what her advice would be, I was doing these things. She said, "Don't do the same thing over and over." She circled me again.

I said, "I thought that was how you got good at something."

She said, "Nope, that's how you get bored with it." Then she smiled again and rose into the biggest, lightest canter maybe I've ever seen, and flew off around the arena. Pie in the Sky's white legs were flashing in the sunshine. I petted Tater and ran my hand through his mane. I said, "Maybe that goes for you, too, Tater boy." And then, while I was watching her, Sophia looped Pie in the Sky to the right and jumped over the rolltop straight out of the arena and galloped down into the forest. I could hear the colonel bark, "Sophia!" and then he marched into the barn as if he had had just about enough, as my grandma would say. Abby stopped to watch from the gate, where she was coming in for my lesson. She said, "You won't believe what she wants to do with that horse."

I said, "What?"

"Take him foxhunting. There's a hunt club up north somewhere. The colonel is—"

"Fit to be tied," I interrupted.

She stared at me for a moment, then laughed. She said, "Yes. Exactly."

"She could take Onyx."

"That would be too easy for Sophia."

"Is foxhunting scary?"

"I've never done it, so I don't really know."

"Has Tater done it?"

"Maybe. He's done a lot of things."

Then, while I was having my lesson and sitting deep and following instructions, I also couldn't help half thinking about what I could do—go on the trail, yes, down to the cove, and along the ocean, and then around and around in an ever-widening circle, looking at everything as I went by it, trotting here, cantering there, walking slowly down a street, and Tater would be turning his head and flicking his ears, but because he is Tater and has already been a lot of places, he would behave himself. It was a nice thought, and every time we followed one of Abby's instructions, it made me feel like if I just did this thing she was telling me to do, I had something to look forward to, and then when I did do that thing, it turned out I *had* had something to look forward to, because that thing she had told me to do was fun, even if it was only coming down to a nice square halt. The reason it was fun was that I could feel Tater right there with me, so smooth and willing, graceful and easygoing. And as I was feeling this, I realized that Tater maybe didn't have much to say, but yes, he was *communicating* with me, and he was letting me *communicate* with him.

I did my turns and my transitions and my halts. Abby put the jumps down to 2'6", and we did three different courses—one more or less a figure eight, one more or less two times around the arena with a loop over the coop in the middle, and one more or less a set of four loops. They weren't perfect—or rather, the first one and the last one weren't perfect, though the middle one was, and I said so and Abby agreed with me—but it was like I knew every step Tater was going to make half a moment before he made it, and somehow that was better than being perfect all the time. I wouldn't have minded if the lesson had gone on all day, but I did feel that Tater was getting tired, so after the third course, I brought him down to the walk, and Abby said, "Do you want to try it again?"

And I said, "Doesn't he have to do another lesson?"

"Yes, after lunch, but he's in good condition, so I don't think—"

"No. He's done fine. I don't want to wear him out."

Abby said, like she wasn't even thinking, "Well, you're the boss."

I said, "Not all the time. But you can say so whenever you like."

We wandered around the arena on a loose rein, and this is the exercise I tried—just looking right or left and shifting my weight in that direction, and sure enough, Tater turned wherever I was looking. After my lesson, I gave him the apple and wished I had about ten of them.

When I came out of the barn, Abby's dad was sitting on the mounting block. He started singing the song, and I listened, but it didn't make any sense to me. I understood the words, or most of the words—"When I was a bachelor, I lived all alone. I worked at the weaver's trade." But then it went on about the girl he marries, and how he keeps her "from the foggy, foggy dew." And then they get married, and then she hides from the foggy, foggy dew, and then it must be that she dies, and then his son reminds him of her, and "of the many, many times that I held her in my arms, just to keep her from the foggy, foggy dew."

I said, "What is the foggy, foggy dew?"

Abby's dad said, "I have no idea."

"And you sing it anyway?"

And he sang it again. I closed my eyes and listened as carefully as I could, even hummed along a little bit, and when we stopped, I sang about half of it. It took me two tries to learn it, and when I was singing it, with my eyes closed, here came Abby's dad, very softly, on the last verse, harmonizing: "He reminds me of the wintertime, part of the summer, too. . . ." When we got to the end, my eyes popped open, and he was smiling. He said, "You don't have to understand something for it to be beautiful. Sometimes the most beautiful things are things that you don't understand."

I said, "Who taught you to sing?"

"Everyone in my family."

And then we sang the song again, because you have to practice, and afterward, I said, "That sounded really good. We did a good job." He patted me on the shoulder, and Abby and Dad came up to us. They didn't clap, but they were smiling, and I think that was better than clapping.

We said good-bye. On the way home, I said to Dad, "Can you teach me to sing?"

"I doubt it. I have a voice like a squawking parrot. Your mom wouldn't even let me sing you a lullaby when you were a baby. Haven't you noticed I don't sing with the radio when we're driving?"

And I hadn't noticed, but now I realized it was true. I said, "That's too bad."

"Well, I love music, though. I'll get out my trumpet

and play a few things, and you can decide if you can stand it or not."

And that's what we did after lunch—Dad got out his trumpet and played three songs, and I could stand it, but I'm not sure about the neighbors, because the trumpet is very loud.

Chapter 16

The next day, Sunday, was very pleasant—warm and bright—and Dad decided it was a perfect day to take Joan Ariel for her first butterfly walk. One interesting thing about our town is that every year a certain kind of butterfly migrates here from Canada and stays for the winter. Grandpa says that the butterflies, which are called monarchs and are very big—orange and black and beautiful—come here for the pines and the eucalyptuses. They cluster in big groups. Once a year, we walk through the trees and look at them. We do projects about them in school, too. Our town is famous for them, and it is interesting that just as the people don't mind the butterflies, the butterflies don't mind the people.

Dad was walking along next to Mom, who was pushing the carriage. Dad had Joan Ariel on his shoulder, and I was walking behind them. When Joan Ariel would look at me, I would make a face until she laughed, and then I would be quiet so that she could look around and maybe see the butterflies. I was thinking about all the things I'd learned the day before, just turning them over in my mind, but that didn't mean I couldn't eavesdrop, and what I heard was Mom saying, "I am so going to miss this."

Dad said, "Why are you going to miss it? We can come here anytime we want to."

"It isn't the same."

So now it was time to interrupt. I jumped around in front of them and stood there. Mom stopped, Dad stopped. I said, "What isn't the same?"

Mom knew exactly what I was talking about, but she didn't say anything. Some people who were also walking stepped around us. They must have been from out of town, because they smiled and said, "Lovely place!"

After that, Dad said, "You didn't tell her?"

I said, "Do you mean me?"

Mom nodded.

"Well, tell me."

Mom said, "Why don't we wait till we get home?"

I said, "Why don't we not wait? I thought everything was settled, and there was going to be a happy ending."

Dad said, "That's only in books."

"What's the sad ending, then?"

Mom walked away from the path, pushing the carriage. I watched her. Dad switched Joan Ariel to his other shoulder, and then she burped a tiny little burp. Dad said, "Okay. Well, you can decide whether it's a sad ending or not."

"What is it?"

"We sold our house because we need the money, and we're going to move right before Christmas."

"Our house? Aunt Johanna's house?"

"Yes."

"Are we moving to Pittsburgh after all?"

"*No!* Forget about Pittsburgh!"

And so I shut up, because even I know that I have to shut up once in a while and make my best effort to *be patient*. So we kept walking among the butterflies, and pretty soon, Mom came back with the carriage, and when she got back, she kissed Joan Ariel first and me second, and by that time, Joan Ariel had fallen asleep, so Dad laid her in the carriage and we walked home, not down the big street and past the stores, but the long way around. Because it was a nice day—no fog and no wind, maybe one of the last really nice days of the year—lots of people were out walking, and of course lots of them knew Mom and Dad, so they said hi and stopped and chatted, and it took us a long time to get home. I wondered who was going to give me the bad news. Mom busied herself with Joan Ariel; Dad mowed our tiny little lawn and then took a shower; and here came Grandma with her casserole pot in her hands. She took it inside and put it in the oven, then went out and sat down in one of the chairs on the front porch, patted the chair next to hers, and said, "Ellen. Come sit beside me for a moment."

I did. And I said nothing. I was listening to myself, and I know that I was not talking.

"Well, it's a little sad, but it's for the best, after all."

Silence.

"Your grandpa's all for it."

Silence.

"We don't want to make too big a deal out of it."

Silence.

"Twenty miles used to be a long way. Amazing

how that's changed, and pretty much entirely in my lifetime."

Silence.

She looked right at me. I said, "Where are we moving?"

"Over there where your dad's new job is. There are some nice houses, really. The landscape is awfully flat, though. Too much sunshine, if you ask me. But people like that."

"Who's moving into our house?"

"Some retired couple from Minnesota. I guess they've been coming here for years, since he was stationed nearby in the war. They heard your mom talking about the garden over at the market, and they came right up to her and said that they've been peeking at the garden for such a long time, it's such a beautiful garden, the wife and the husband both love to garden, they have lilacs and roses and apple trees, but after all, it is Minnesota, and your mom invited them to have a real look, and lo and behold, they made an offer, and it was a good offer, too. And I know—now that Joan Ariel is here, your family is about to burst out of this place, it is tiny, but even so . . ." And then she sighed.

I got up and gave her a good hug, and also a kiss,

because I did not want her to know that the very first thought I had about moving was that I absolutely could not wait, because why would I not want to be closer to Tater and Ned and Abby? So here is another kind of secret—the kind that might hurt somebody's feelings if you tell it.

It turned out that not only had Dad been looking at cars, he had been looking at houses, because on the following Saturday, he "suggested" that I get ready for my lesson first thing because he wanted to leave early, and then Mom and Joan Ariel got into the car with us and we were out of the driveway before the fog had even begun to lift. Joan Ariel was in the car seat, and I watched her. She likes to look out of the window, even at her age, which I think is interesting. I decided that she was going to be a mountain climber, and then I named some mountains in my mind, but only ones with interesting names: Kilimanjaro, Olympus, Matterhorn. I thought that when we got home, I would sit Joan Ariel on my lap and we would look for them in the atlas. We drove up the hill, through Monterey, out into the valley. The fog became sunshine. We did not turn down the road that leads to Abby's place, but went on toward our new town. We passed some stores, then turned left and right, and there we were, driving slowly down a wide, flat street. The houses looked new, and there were some empty lots. There were trees, but they were small, like they had just been planted. The ocean was nowhere to be seen. Then, just a little farther on, the neighborhood changed—the houses were older, some with pointed roofs and some that looked Spanish—and then, after what seemed like just a moment, the neighborhood changed again. Joan Ariel had fallen asleep and Mom wasn't saying anything, just looking here and there as we turned a corner and then turned another corner. I saw that it was going to be hard to choose a house. We drove past a school. It, too, was long and flat, with a tower at one end. Everything in this new town was different. It gave me a weird feeling. But then I remembered that Abby must have gone to this school, and she would know all about it. I looked at my watch and spoke up. I said, "It's ten o'clock. My lesson is at ten-thirty." Yes, I sounded like a schoolteacher.

That was the first step, and I am here to tell you that moving out of your house to another one, even if it is the very one you want in the very spot you like best, is a step-by-step process, and about ten times a day you say to yourself, "Why are we doing this? Do I really have to throw out all of these clothes, and do I really have to fold all the other ones very neatly and stick them in a box, and where is that blouse Mom bought me in the spring—did I throw it away? Do I really have to choose between a nice modern flat house and a nice old-fashioned two-story house that cost about the same?" And I admit that this wasn't actually my choice, but I did have an opinion, and Mom and Dad should have let me vote.

And the other thing was that all of a sudden, Joan Ariel started crawling, and it was like one day she sat up and moved forward a little bit and the next day she was a racehorse, going all over the house, and we had to watch the stairs and the doors. But Joan Ariel wasn't about to fall down the stairs. She would set herself at the top and stare and stare, and then, all on her own, she figured out how to turn around and go down knees first. Then she figured out how to go back up, and then Grandma said, "Well, she is a runner."

I said, "What's that?"

"Oh, my goodness, a baby or a toddler who is just determined to get out of town."

I must have looked shocked when she said that,

because she looked at me and laughed and said, "Of course I'm exaggerating, but some kids, when they figure out how to move, they want to move all the time, and faster and faster."

"Was I a runner?"

"No, and thank goodness. You were a looker. If you were sitting by a window and suddenly turned your head, I would go over and try to see what you were looking at, and it was always something—a man walking up the street, or a squirrel on the porch, or even a bird. Always something. We didn't have to chase you. When you went somewhere, you always acted like you knew just where you were going." And then she followed Joan Ariel into the dining room and stayed with her while she crawled round and round the table.

After all, it was good that they didn't give me the deciding vote, because another house came on the market all of a sudden and we all liked it, including Grandma, who visited it and said she would stay with us anytime we pleased, and that was the one we moved into. It was right on the corner between a sunny street and a shady street, across from a park for Joan Ariel to run around in, and walking distance (*flat* walking distance) from all the schools. After our old house, it seemed so big that you could ride a bike inside, but when I said that (and I was serious), Mom just laughed. It was two stories (the second story only had two bedrooms) and had a fenced backyard, with a patio that Joan Ariel could crawl around on and plenty of room for a garden.

Yes, it was step by step, and then it all sped up. We had Thanksgiving dinner at Grandma and Grandpa's because everything at our place was pretty much packed, and then on the first day of Christmas break, which was a Thursday, the movers came and put everything in their giant truck and moved it all to the new house. In six days, Mom, Grandma, and Grandpa got the house set up (we slept on the floor only the first night, and it was fun), and I did go to Abby's ranch for a lesson that Saturday and I timed the drive—twelve minutes. When we got there, I said to Dad that I loved our new house, and he said, "Me too. Room to stretch out," and I saw that I didn't have to keep my secret anymore. I didn't know what I wanted for Christmas— I couldn't think of a single thing.

Epilogue

On Christmas morning, I woke up early, as always. In the new house, the light was already bright, not because the sun comes up earlier (I asked Mom), but because the hills don't hide it. The window of my room faces west, and there are trees, but if I sit up and look out the window, I can see lots of sky. I waited for a cloud and not a single one showed up. I got up and went downstairs. The Christmas tree was small this year. We'd gotten it the previous afternoon—the last one on the lot—and brought it home. We had decorated it after Joan Ariel fell asleep, so when I got into the living room, I had to smile at the way she was sitting there, completely quiet, just looking and looking at the tree. I guess it seemed big to her. I went over to it and shook my presents—only a few. But what did I want? I still didn't know, and I didn't know if the new house had cost so much money that it was our real Christmas present.

About an hour later, Grandma and Grandpa showed up for breakfast, with coffee cake and ambrosia and a plate of frosted sugar cookies. When I unwrapped the boxes, I found a new hard hat for riding and a thick book about a wrinkle in time, which I looked at for about a minute until I saw another book under the tree called *All About Horses*. And there was a sweater. From Grandma, there is always a sweater, because she loves to knit. Joan Ariel's sweater was yellow and mine was red. I kissed her and thanked her for it not being pink.

It looked like Christmas Day was going to last a long time. Not even noon yet. I was so bored that I went into the kitchen, found a dishcloth, and started helping with the dishes. Mom kept washing and rinsing and didn't say anything. When we were done, she swept the floor and I held the dustpan. When the kitchen looked sparkly clean, I said, "It's pretty warm. I think I'll walk over to the park."

"You could do that," said Mom. When I was just

about in the doorway to the dining room, she went on, "But we have something else to do first."

In the living room, Grandma, Grandpa, Dad, and Joan Ariel were already waiting beside the door. Dad had my jacket in his hand. I said, "We have a house. We chose this house. We don't need to look at any others."

Dad laughed and the others smiled. But I didn't say anything more. I just took my jacket and put it on. We went out and got into the car, and it was a pretty tight fit. It took me about three minutes to realize that we were not going to the nearby market (which was closed, but looked enormous and delicious). At that corner, when we turned right, I realized we were going to Abby's ranch, and everyone in the car, except maybe Joan Ariel, knew why we were going there. I looked around. Dad and Grandpa were talking about Fords and Chevrolets, and Mom and Grandma were talking about pacifiers. I put my hand over my mouth to hide my smile and didn't say a single word. I really didn't. I knew that I only had to keep my new secret for eight more minutes.

The gate at Abby's ranch was wide open. We drove

in, and as soon as Dad turned the car off, Abby came running out with Rusty at her heels (Rusty was not barking—she was wagging her tail), and then came Abby's dad and then her mom. Abby gave me a hug and ran off.

Everyone was now out of our car. Grandma was holding Joan Ariel, who was yawning. Mom came over and said, "You need this, sweetie," and she pulled a bandanna out of her pocket and tied it gently over my eyes. Then she turned me around like it was a game of hide-and-seek, then I heard some clip-clopping and Abby's dad singing "Joy to the World." He got through one verse before Mom pulled off the bandanna, and there was Tater right in front of me, with his ears pricked, so that he looked very handsome, and then he reached his nose forward and sniffed my hand (always polite) and nickered, and that was what told me he was now my horse, my Christmas present, and I wondered when Grandma was going to exclaim, "Where in the world did you get that kind of money!" but I said nothing, and I put my arms around Tater's neck gently, and I gave him a kiss on the cheek, and then everyone said, "Merry Christmas!" and Joan Ariel started to cry because she was hungry, and probably also because she wanted to get down on the ground and explore the farm, and I was glad she became the center of attention, because really, I just wanted to stand there, holding Tater's lead rope in my hand and petting his shining neck and thinking about what it feels like that very moment when you get what you have wanted for as long as you can remember.

About the Author

Jane Smiley is the author of many books for adults, including *Some Luck, Horse Heaven,* and the Pulitzer Prize–winning *A Thousand Acres.* She was inducted into the American Academy of Arts and Letters in 2001. The first book in the Ellen & Ned trilogy was *Riding Lessons.* She is also the author of five Horses of Oak Valley Ranch books, *The Georges and the Jewels, A Good Horse, True Blue, Pie in the Sky,* and *Gee Whiz.*

Jane Smiley lives in Northern California, where she rides horses every chance she gets.